Power
Play

Alan Gi██████ ██me writer and a visiting speaker and lecturer
at schoo██ ████████ literary events nationwide, including the major
book fe████ ████ ██h, Northern Children's Book Festival, Swansea,
Chelten ——————— ── d Salford. Alan has recently embarked on a high
profile, nationwide campaign to champion libraries and librarianship and
to reevaluate government commitment to educational spending.

Also by Alan Gibbons:

FOOTBALL TITLES
Julie and Me and Michael Owen Makes Three
Total Football series:
Some You Win . . .
Under Pressure
Divided We Fall
Injury Time
Last Man Standing
Twin Strikers
Final Countdown

HORROR TITLES
Hell's Underground:
Scared to Death
The Demon Assassin
Renegade
Witch Breed

FANTASY TITLES
The Legendeer Trilogy:
Shadow of the Minotaur
Vampyr Legion
Warriors of the Raven

The Legendeer Trilogy (3-in-1)

The Darkwing:
Rise of the Blood Moon
Setting of a Cruel Sun

The Darkwing Omnibus (2-in-1)

REAL LIFE THRILLERS
The Lost Boys' Appreciation Society
Blood Pressure
The Edge
Caught in the Crossfire
The Defender

Power
Play

Alan Gibbons

Orion
Children's Books

First published in Great Britain in 1998
by Orion Children's Books
Reissued in Great Britain in 2010
by Orion Children's Books
a division of the Orion Publishing Group Ltd
Orion House
5 Upper St Martin's Lane
London WC2H 9EA
An Hachette UK company

978-1-4440-0178-5

A catalogue record for this book is available from the British Library.

www.orionbooks.co.uk

Rough Diamonds

THE SQUAD

Darren 'Daz' Kemble (goalkeeper)
Joey Bannen (defence)
Anthony 'Ant' Glover (defence)
Gordon Jones (defence)
Jimmy Mintoe (defence)
Bashir Gulaid (midfield)
John O'Hara (midfield)
Kevin 'Guv' McGovern (midfield and captain)
Pete 'Ratso' Ratcliffe (midfield)
Jamie Moore (striker)
Conor Savage (striker)
Dougie Long (utility player and substitute
goalkeeper)
Liam Savage (utility player)

Manager: Ronnie Mintoe

PART ONE

The Fire Inside

One

'Who's that?'

An innocent enough question, you don't think? It's what I asked my cousin Cheryl the first time I saw Chris Power. But it was a question I would have to go on asking. It didn't matter how much I found out about him, I still didn't really know who he was, or quite what made him tick. Not until the very end, and then it was almost too late. He remained a stranger, which is pretty weird really when you consider how much alike we are, me and Chris. I suppose that's why I took such an immediate interest in him. It was his anger. I felt it straight away, like a charge running between us. Anger's the energy I've run on most of my life. Anger that my dad cleared off on us four years ago. Anger that me, Mum and my divvy brother Gareth have ended up stuck all on our own on a lousy estate like the Diamond. Anger that when he resurfaced Dad was no hero returning from the dead like I'd always imagined, just a beat-up ex-boxer who was ready to hire out his fists to the highest bidder. And the highest bidder had to be a scumbag local villain by the name of Lee Ramage. He has this taxi firm on South Parade – a real hooky outfit I bet. The trouble is my mate Bashir's dad has the shop next door and Ramage doesn't like the idea. Thinks he might blow him up to the police, I bet. He's been trying to put Mr Gulaid out of business, and using Dad to do it. Having to choose between your dad and your mate – like I said, I know all about anger. That's why I was drawn to Chris, because of the rage I could sense within him. He's like me. So much like me sometimes that it's like looking in a mirror. But there's one big difference. I've got it under control, all that *anger and fire inside me. It was a struggle, but I really do think I've done it. That's what makes me the Guv'nor. I've learned to use it, channel it.*

There was a time when I'd do anything to hit back at the world: fight, spit, bite, smash things, set fires. Yes, especially set fires. That was a cute little habit that sent my life into free fall for a while. Not any more, I was at a crossroads. Either I found something to rebuild my life around, or I ended up walking the same crooked road as Dad. Well, I made my choice and that's down to football.

For the last twelve months I've been captain of a side in the South Sefton Junior League, the Rough Diamonds. So all this rage that builds up in me, all the fire I feel licking away, I put it into my game. Like I said, I'm the Guv'nor. My team's hard as nails, but skilful with it. The Beast with a bit of Beauty thrown in.

That's how we turned things round last season, starting out as licking boys and ending up as Challenge Cup winners. We had fire in our bellies, but we learned discipline too. Which is where Chris would turn out to be so different. When I feel the pressure building up I focus it, like one of those laser beams. I concentrate it, close on my target. Then – bam! – I win. Not Chris. He just blows – and how! He's like a box of fireworks all going off at the same time. The trouble is, the last time he blew it looked like it would wreck everything. The Diamonds' season, my dreams of a future in football, our whole lives.

Bam! – we lose.

Two

'Who's that?' Kev McGovern nodded in the direction of the boy emerging from Cheryl's front door.

'Oh,' said Cheryl, nervously twisting a lock of hair, 'that's Chris.'

Kev inspected him from a distance. They were about the same age. Same sort of build too, except Chris was slightly thinner and less robust looking. 'Chris who?'

'Power. His name's Power.' There was a flatness about Cheryl's voice, but it didn't put Kev off the scent. It just made him more curious. His attention shifted from the crop-haired boy in his Puma King jacket to a tall bespectacled woman saying goodbye to Cheryl's parents.

'And her?'

'Mrs Burrows. I thought you might already know her.'

Kev frowned. 'Know her? Why should I?'

'She's a social worker. Like Willy.'

Kev drew in his breath. He hated being reminded of Willy – Mrs Williams to everybody else. She'd been in charge of him the time he got into trouble for the fires. It was ancient history, that awful summer on the old estate, but somehow it had a knack of coming back to haunt him. He'd got away to the sprawling 1960s housing development that was the Diamond, but he hadn't been able to leave his nightmares behind.

'What's a social worker doing round yours?' demanded Kev anxiously. His flesh was creeping. Did it have something to do with him? But how could it? He'd kept his nose clean for months. Besides, why would they come sniffing round his aunty's of all people?

'Nothing to worry about,' said Cheryl with an understanding smile. 'It hasn't got anything to do with you. It's about us.'

'You?' Kev couldn't believe his ears. Uncle Dave and aunty Pat were the original Mr and Mrs Straight.

As for Cheryl, she was such a Goody-Two-Shoes, sainthood must be just around the corner. So why the social worker?

Cheryl took a deep breath. 'Mum and Dad have decided to foster.'

'What, take kids in, you mean?'

'That's it.'

Mrs Burrows ushered Chris Power into her car, then got in herself. Kev glanced at Cheryl.

'So how come you never said anything before?' No answer, just a noncommittal shrug of the shoulders.

'You're not keen, are you?' he asked. The car pulled away.

'No,' Cheryl admitted. 'I'm not. I don't know why they want to invite some strange kid into the house. Things are fine as they are.'

'So who is this Chris guy anyway?' asked Kev. 'What happened to his own family?'

'I'm not sure really,' Cheryl answered. 'Mum and Dad are a bit cagey over it. All I know is he's in care. He's in a children's home on the Drive. One of those big houses near the flyover.'

Kev was interested. No, more than interested, intrigued. He watched the car turn towards Rice Lane. 'So when does all this happen? When does he move in?'

Cheryl nudged a discarded polystyrene chip-tray with her toe. 'Never, I hope.'

'But if it does?'

Cheryl sighed. 'Nothing's sorted yet.' She looked in her parents' direction. 'At least it *wasn't*.'

'Oh, hi there,' called aunty Pat, spotting them. 'Did you have a nice time?'

Jamie had gone out for the day with his mum and Bashir was helping in the family shop, so for want of mates Kev had tagged along with Cheryl to the Superbowl. Cheryl and her loopy friend Helen, the one who had a stupid crush on him.

'So where's Helen?' asked uncle Dave. 'I thought she'd still be in tow, considering Kev's still around.'

Kev smiled at the gentle ribbing. 'Her dad's birthday. She had to go home … *thank goodness.*'

Cheryl joined in the teasing. 'But you like her really.'

'Behave,' retorted Kev, getting hot under the collar. 'She does my head in.'

'You won't be saying that in a couple of years,' said aunty Pat. 'Anyway, do you want your tea here? A butty or something?'

Kev was about to make his excuses and head for home when he remembered Chris Power. 'I wouldn't mind,' he said. 'I'll ring Mum and let her know where I am.'

Kev had just replaced the receiver when he heard aunty Pat's voice in the kitchen. 'There's no need to take that attitude, Cheryl.'

Then his cousin's sulky retort: 'I'm not taking an attitude.'

'Not much,' said uncle Dave. 'All we're asking is for you to give the lad a chance. He hasn't had the easiest start in life. You wouldn't want him to stay in care, would you?'

Kev sidled quietly into the living-room. He was enjoying himself. It made a welcome change for Cheryl's side of the family to have rows. The Taskers never had much difficulty keeping their noses clean – not like the McGoverns. The Taskers had it all. Uncle Dave was a steady bloke with a job and everything. Not like Kev's dad, a wheeler-dealer and King Rat to most people on the estate. Then there were Mum and aunty

Pat. They were twin sisters but Mum chain-smoked and looked ten years older. The Taskers, Kev sometimes thought, were just too nice for their own good. So when he inspected Cheryl's pouting face he couldn't help gloating a bit.

'Why us, though?' she asked. 'Why can't somebody else take him in?'

'They could,' said aunty Pat. 'But we *want* to do it. I thought you'd understand.'

Cheryl noticed Kev watching her. 'I don't know what you're staring at,' she snapped. Kev gave a superior smile. He was revelling in her discomfort all right.

'Ignore our Cheryl,' uncle Dave advised. 'She has these little tantrums.'

'I'm not having a tantrum!' said Cheryl indignantly. 'I just don't see what he's got to move in here for. Ugh, that stupid bonehead haircut!'

'Now that's enough,' said aunty Pat, her patience beginning to fray. 'Chris is coming to us and that's that.'

'And I don't get a say?'

'Oh, I think you've had your say,' snorted uncle Dave. 'More than once. Now, can we get on with our tea in peace?'

'You eat your tea,' said Cheryl abruptly. 'I'm going to my room. Or maybe you're thinking of moving lodgers in there too!' With that she stamped upstairs. As her bedroom door slammed shut aunty Pat sighed and turned to Kev.

'Chicken burger on a bun do you, Kev?'

'Yes,' Kev replied. 'That'd be smashing. So what's Cheryl so hot and bothered about?' Aunty Pat and uncle Dave exchanged glances. They didn't look too keen to let him in on it.

'Cheryl likes her privacy,' said aunty Pat. 'You can understand it, I suppose. Only child, and all that.'

'Spoilt, you mean?' asked Kev, all mock innocence. He was enjoying twisting the knife.

'Anyway,' said uncle Dave, clapping his hands briskly. He was announcing the end of the discussion about Chris Power. 'How's things with the Diamonds?'

'OK,' said Kev. He didn't intend to get side-tracked.

'Who are you playing tomorrow?'

'Fix-It DIY.'

'Are they good?'

'Not really,' said Kev, gulping down a mouthful of chicken. 'We took four points off them last season. Thrashed them six–two in one game.'

'So you're optimistic?'

'Aren't I always?' Kev became aware of aunty Pat smiling. That's when he realized. Uncle Dave had done it. He'd got him right off the subject. Kev had another shot at bringing up Chris Power.

'Does this Chris lad like footy?'

Uncle Dave looked wary. 'Dunno really. It hasn't come up.'

'He might though, mightn't he? I could take him down South Road and introduce him to the Diamonds.'

Suddenly aunty Pat wasn't smilng. She liked Kev but not enough to trust him with Chris. Like giving a bull a china shop to mind. 'Don't go planning too much for him,' she said. 'He won't even be moving in for two or three weeks.'

'How come?'

'That's just the way it is,' said uncle Dave. 'Red tape, I dare say. Now, do you want a lift home?' Kev knew when people were trying to get rid of him.

'That's all right,' he replied. 'I'll walk.'

'Sure?'

'Positive. Say goodbye to Cheryl for me.' As he sauntered down the street of neatly refurbished turn-of-the-century houses towards the grim disrepair of the Diamond, Kev remembered something about Chris Power. It was the way he walked, wound up, bristling with resentment. And the scowl on his face, he remembered that too.

'We're brothers all right,' Kev told himself. 'Brothers under the skin.'

Three

Mrs Burrows squinted against the strong early autumn sunlight. 'Nice people, the Taskers,' she said, pulling into the kerb.

'If you say so.' Chris wasn't in the mood to reassure the old bat that he was happy with the arrangement. What was the big deal anyway? They were getting paid to take him in. So what made them nice? Just another set of do-gooders shoving their noses in where they weren't wanted. Besides, it would probably fall through anyway. Things usually did.

'You are happy with the move?' Mrs Burrows asked, releasing her seat-belt.

'Don't mind.' That's it, he thought, keep it neutral. Hide the fact that he quite liked the look of the foster parents. Dare to hope and you only get knocked down. It's the law of the land.

'But it's better than here,' she continued. 'You'll have your own room. No more sharing.'

Sure, thought Chris, it had that going for it. No more Crusty picking at his arms and rabbiting away to himself half the night. No more having his stuff pinched. Crusty wasn't too bad as room-mates go, but he wasn't half light-fingered.

'When do I go?' asked Chris.

'By the end of the month, I should think,' Mrs Burrows replied. 'Early October at the latest. Looking forward to it?'

Don't push it, thought Chris.

'Anyway,' said Mrs Burrows, opening the car door. 'I'd better get you back.'

Chris grunted. She must think I'm going to turn into Cinderella or something.

'Oh, and Chris. Don't …'

Reading her mind, he slammed the door with all his might. The whole car shook. 'Don't what?'

Mrs Burrows pressed the key-fob alarm and gave a sigh of resignation.

'It doesn't matter.' Chris smiled to himself. Do-gooders, he loved getting into their cars. He played with all the gadgets and treated everything as roughly as he could. It was a performance he'd just about perfected, the octopus-armed kid from hell. And didn't it get them on edge! Still, they could take it. At least they had cars. They had everything. What did he have? A dad in a cell and a mum so far away she might as well be on another planet.

Mrs Burrows led the way round to the front door. She tapped on the window and smiled at Gerwyn. 'Here's Chris,' she announced.

'And I thought it was Duncan Ferguson,' joked Gerwyn, letting them in.

Chris kept his face straight. He quite liked Gerwyn, but he tried not to let it show too often. It was pointless getting to like anybody. They always moved on, leaving him on his own again.

'I suppose you want to know how the Blues are getting on?' said Gerwyn.

Of course he did. Dave Tasker was a Blue and he'd had the Everton game on at the start of the visit. Then just as they started to come under the cosh he'd turned it off to talk. The moment Chris got in the car he tried to tune Mrs Burrows' radio into City Sport, but she'd thought he was messing again and switched it off. That really got him but he didn't let on. He'd got used to suffering in silence.

Gerwyn laughed off Chris's deliberate snub. 'Always enthusiastic, our Chris,' he joked.

'So what's the score?' asked Chris. His insides were churning. They couldn't be losing. Not to Coventry.

'They're one–nil down, I'm afraid.'

Chris consulted his watch. 'Twenty minutes into the second half.' His voice changed, assuming a wounded urgency. 'Come on Blues.'

'I've got the match on in the kitchen,' said Gerwyn. 'Fancy listening to it with me? Cook's off ill so I'm cutting a few butties. I could do with some company.'

'S'all right,' said Chris. 'I'll listen to it in my room.'

Gerwyn looked disappointed. 'Fair enough. Don't go winding up Crusty though.'

'*Me* wind *him* up. Joking aren't you?'

'See you soon, Chris,' said Mrs Burrows as he jogged upstairs. He heard but he didn't answer. What did she expect, hearts and flowers?

'You there, Crusty?' asked Chris, shoving the door open. Crusty stood up abruptly, which usually meant he'd been messing with Chris's stuff.

'What are you doing?' asked Chris.

'Nothing.'

'What've you got in your hand?'

'Nothing.'

'Come on. Cough.' Crusty edged to the window. 'Show me your hands.'

'Why should I?'

Chris was losing his temper. 'Because I'll burst you if you don't.'

Crusty opened his fist and let something drop through the open window.

'What was that?' Chris pushed Crusty out of the way.

'What did you throw outside?' Crusty made for the door. He'd only taken a couple of steps when Chris caught sight of his radio-cassette lying on Crusty's bed. The lead was missing. 'You've robbed the plug and lead, haven't you?' Crusty made a break for the door. 'You thieving get!' yelled Chris, throwing himself across the room. 'And I was just going to listen to the match.'

'Gerroff!' shrieked Crusty. Frankie 'Crusty' Cobb was fourteen but acted like he was eight. He was also scared witless of the younger boy. He'd been the butt of his temper more than once. Carried forward by their momentum the boys crashed on to the landing.

'I wanted to listen to the Blues. They've got their backs against the wall. Now you've ruined it, you thieving rat.'

'Gerroff!' squealed Crusty. 'I never took your stupid lead.'

Chris sat on Crusty's chest. 'Yes you did. I know you did. Now go and get it for me.'

'Won't!'

Chris gripped Crusty's chin and pressed hard. 'You will, you know.'

'No way.'

Chris heard footsteps on the stairs but he didn't ease

up. 'Either you do it the easy way or I kick you all the way there.'

'Chris!' It was Gerwyn's voice. 'What's going on here?'

'He's been at it again,' roared Chris. 'He can't keep his hands off my stuff. I told him what I'd do to him if he tried it again.'

'Let him up,' said Gerwyn.

'Only if he gets my lead.'

'*I'll* go for the lead,' said Gerwyn. 'On one condition.'

'What's that?'

'You don't touch Crusty.'

Chris stared back with cold eyes. 'All right.'

'Promise you won't lay a hand on him?'

'I told you, didn't I?'

'Right,' said Gerwyn. 'I'll get your lead.'

Chris waited until Gerwyn was out of earshot then punched Crusty in the ribs. Hard.

'But you promised,' gasped Crusty, the tears starting in his eyes.

'Grow up, Crusty,' said Chris. 'Who keeps promises? Nobody's ever done it for me. So why should I start?'

Crusty didn't offer an answer. There wasn't one.

Four

Sunday morning early, and the Diamonds were getting changed, ready for the third game of the season.

'It's all right,' said Liam Savage. 'I don't mind being sub.'

Kev shook his head. That's why Liam's twin brother

Conor had got the nod over him. That little bit more aggression, that extra dash of determination. It was something Kev had noticed already, and the twins had only been around for a week or so. Liam always deferred to Conor. He wondered what it was like having a twin brother. Better in some ways. You'd have the same interests, being the same age and all. But did you ever have any time to yourself? At least he could bar Gareth from his room.

'Well, I *do* mind,' protested Dougie Long, crossing the changing rooms to make his point. 'What good is sub? Why him instead of me?'

'Because,' Ronnie Mintoe told him, 'Conor ran that little five-a-side on Friday night. Best player on the park. Play for your place, son. We've got a bit of a squad now, and there are no automatic choices any more.'

'But I joined the Diamonds before he did,' argued Dougie petulantly. He too was new to the Diamonds and he was unfamiliar with the manager's methods.

'Oh, knock it off, Dougie,' said Kev. 'Ronnie's right ...'

'Oh, I'm right, Kev,' said Ronnie, running his fingers through his greying hair, 'And I don't need your help explaining it to Dougie, thank you very much.' The reprimand was delivered with unexpected venom. It seemed out of character somehow.

'Touchy,' Kev said to Jamie. Ronnie's words had stung him and he was finding it hard to disguise the fact.

'Keep it down, Guv,' warned Jamie. 'Ronnie's looking this way.'

'All right, Ron?' asked Kev brightly.

'I'll be better when you learn to button your lip,' Ronnie replied frostily.

'Which side of the bed did he get out of this morning?' Kev whispered.

'The wrong side,' said Jamie, smiling.

'When we're quite ready,' said Ronnie. 'We've a match to get ready for.' Kev scratched his nose. Who needed reminding? Same every Sunday morning, scurrying round Jacob's Lane playing field fighting for glory. 'We've had a reasonable start to the season,' Ronnie continued. 'One win, one defeat, and that was against quality opposition. But we can do better, lads, especially now that we've extended the squad.' The other boys glanced at newcomers Dougie Long who'd played in the first two games and the Savage twins who had yet to make their debut. 'You turned this lot over in good style at the end of last season.'

'Six–two,' said Ratso, interrupting. He was the team's Statto, a master statistician with an encyclopaedic knowledge of soccer trivia.

'Yes, thank you Peter,' said Ronnie tetchily, 'I am aware of our results.'

'Sorry for breathing,' said Ratso. Kev and Jamie exchanged glances. Ronnie was definitely in a mood.

'So go out and hammer them,' Ronnie concluded, glancing at his watch. 'That's it.' A murmur ran through the players. That must be Ronnie's shortest team talk ever.

'What's with Ronnie today?' asked Ant.

'Beats me,' said Daz. 'Do you know, Jimmy?' Jimmy was Ronnie's nephew. The rest of the team had come to expect privileged information.

'Not really,' said Jimmy. 'He was dead quiet on the way up in the car. But he was on a shout last night. Maybe he's just tired.'

'A shout,' said Ant. 'What the heck's that?'

'Don't they have telly in your house?' asked Jimmy.

'A shout. You know. Firemen. Hoses. Nee-naw. Nine-nine-nine.'

'All right, all right,' said Ant. 'I get the point. So Ronnie was fighting a fire, was he?'

Ant's words were the cue for Ronnie to walk back into the changing room. 'Are you playing this morning, or what?' he demanded. 'Fix-It are on the pitch already. Raring to go. I wish I could say the same for you lot.'

'Is he always like this?' asked Liam Savage apprehensively.

'No,' joked Ratso. 'He's worse sometimes.'

Once on the pitch the Diamonds forgot their manager's grumbling. No sooner had the referee got the match underway than the Diamonds settled into their usual game, harrying and getting in tight. John Merton had the ball for Fix-It, but was immediately closed down by three players. Hurrying his pass he let Jamie in on the edge of the penalty area. Looking for support, Jamie played the ball inside to Conor whose shot was parried by the keeper only to be fizzed back in by Kev. He watched in anguish as his shot cannoned off the upright.

'Well played,' Kev told Conor.

'It's always well played with me,' said Conor.

'Cocky beggar, isn't he?' Kev said to Jamie.

'Remind you of anyone, Guv?' asked Jamie. Kev just smiled. Two minutes later the ball was with Conor again. He brought it down, clipped it into the middle and picked up the return ball in a left-wing position.

'Conor,' shouted Jamie, making a run, but Conor wasn't interested. Instead he knocked the ball back to John O'Hara and drove forward into the Fix-It defence, expecting the return pass.

'John,' shouted Jamie hopefully, but again he was overlooked.

Checking, John laid the ball out to Bashir on the left. Scurrying to control it, Bashir set off on a line-hugging run. He was fifteen yards from the goal line. Suddenly he had all sorts of options. Jamie and Conor were both shouting his name as they closed on goal, but Bashir was more interested in Kev coming in at the far post.

'Bash!' yelled Kev. Bashir obliged and Kev nodded home from close range. One–nil.

'I was in a better position,' grumbled Conor.

'Guv scored, didn't he?' said Jamie.

'Yes, I suppose so.'

'Could be a problem that,' observed Kev once Conor was safely out of earshot.

'How do you mean?' asked Jamie.

'Conor,' said Kev. 'A bit selfish, isn't he?'

Jamie nodded. 'Just a bit. Still, it's early days. He needs time to settle in.'

Fix-It remained on the back foot from the restart. It was almost as if they were scared of the Diamonds after their sparkling opening.

'Step it up, lads,' said Kev, encouraging his team. 'We're going to take this shower to the cleaners.'

As if to prove Kev's prediction, Jimmy took possession midway in his own half and transferred play to the left. Bashir knocked it inside to Ratso and set off on the overlap. Seeing the Fix-It defenders doubling up on the little winger, Ratso looked for a free man and found him in Jamie Moore running wide. Jamie took on Neil Black, the Fix-It fullback and burst into the penalty area. With the keeper coming out to narrow the angle, Jamie whipped the ball in dangerously. It evaded Kev and John, but Conor was on hand to tap it home. Two–nil.

'Nice one,' shouted Jamie, giving Conor the thumbs up.

'I know,' said Conor as he swaggered towards the halfway line.

'The boy's a cauliflower,' said Kev.

'Come again?'

'Big-head.'

'Oh yeah,' said Jamie, smiling, 'Not half.'

Just before half-time the Diamonds went further ahead. This time Joey Bannen was the play-maker. Tracking back to give cover he won the ball on the edge of his own penalty area and brought it out of defence. Finding himself in oceans of space, Joey dribbled it across the halfway line and played it to Bashir who had space to move it infield. Looking up, Bashir played it in towards the edge of the area where Jamie was on hand to flick it into the unmarked Conor. Conor swivelled and hammered it home on the half-volley. Three–nil.

'Now that,' said Conor, striding across the box with his arms raised, 'Is what you call finishing.'

'And that,' Jamie murmured behind his back, 'Is what you call a big-head.'

'Yes,' said Kev, beginning to reconsider his previous judgement, 'But he's a good big-head.'

The turnaround was complete. Just as Kev began to warm to the new addition, Jamie was having doubts.

After half-time it was backs-to-the-wall for Fix-It as the Diamonds ran riot. Conor completed his hat trick with a glancing header at the far post. Five minutes later Bashir got in on the scoring beating three players before sliding the ball home under the goalie's body.

'This,' breathed Kev ecstatically, 'Is what Sundays are for.'

'Too right,' said Jamie, 'And there's more to come.'

It took ten minutes to confirm the prophecy and it was Bashir who again unlocked the Fix-It defence with a dizzying run that turned two defenders inside out before he released the ball to Jamie. Seizing on the chance, he drove into the area only to be floored by the keeper.

Penalty.

'It's all yours, Jay,' said Kev, then glimpsing movement to his right: 'Hey, what do you think you're doing?'

Conor had snatched up the ball and was heading for the spot. 'You've seen how I can finish,' he said. 'I'm taking it.'

'Over my dead body,' said Kev, grabbing at the ball.

'Fair enough,' said Conor, facing up to Kev. 'If that's how you want it.'

Kev looked towards the touch line. 'Ronnie,' he called. 'Get him off.'

'What?' barked Ronnie. 'Oh, give me a break. Can't you sort it yourself?'

'Oh, I'll sort it all right,' said Kev. 'Drop that ball or you're off.'

'Me?' cried Conor. 'You can't take me off. I've scored a hat trick.'

'And if you don't toe the line,' said Kev. 'It'll be your last for us. I'm the skipper and I say Jamie takes it. If you want to argue go and do it with Ronnie.' It was a disgruntled Conor who reluctantly released the ball.

'Still want him off?' asked Ronnie.

'Nah,' said Kev. 'It's sorted. He can stay.'

Jamie converted the penalty to make it six–nil but there was a shadow over the result.

'Keep an eye on that one, Guv,' said Jamie, nodding in Conor's direction.

'Don't worry,' said Kev as the final whistle blew. 'I will.'

Five

Ronnie wasn't half short with me today. I just don't get it. It's like I've done something. But what? I played my heart out. As per usual. And took the reins on the pitch. As per usual. And took the difficult decisions. As per usual. But did he have a kind word? Did he heck. I went across to talk to Conor but Ronnie cut me dead. He didn't want to know. He just carried on talking to Daz Kemble's old man. You'd think I wasn't there. So what's with him? We've had our moments but most of the time we get on. All of a sudden I'm being frozen out. Weird. After a six–nil victory I should have been walking on air. Instead, I came away feeling really flat.

Ronnie wasn't the only reason, either. For a start, there were my old enemies Brain Damage – yes, that's Lee Ramage's kid brother – and Costello. They'd just finished on one of the other pitches. They'd won as well. They were dead mouthy about it. Usually, I'd have given as good as I got, reminding them that we'd battered them in the second game of the season, but after the way Ronnie had been with me I just wasn't in the mood.

Then to cap it all, there's something else. It's my Everton shirt, the one Mum bought me last birthday. It's gone missing. I can't bring myself to tell her. She had to go without for weeks to afford that shirt. I know how hard she tries to give me and Gareth the stuff other kids get. This was a mega-present. Now it's gone. I've been wracking my brains. I went to the Liver Bird game in it last week, but I must have left it somewhere when I got changed. It wasn't in my locker with my other gear so I had to leave my match shirt on. I didn't give it much thought at the time. Besides, Mum wanted me home sharpish that day and I couldn't hang around. I assumed it had fallen down the back of the radiator or something.

I thought it would turn up but I've searched everywhere and I've asked the ground staff and the caretaker and nobody's seen it.

What makes me mad is, it's no use to anybody else. It's got my name monogrammed on the back. Who in their right mind would walk around with my name plastered across their back?

Typical, isn't it? I just wonder what's going to be next.

Six

The next disaster wasn't long in coming. The moment Kev got in from the match Mum met him at the door.

'What have you been up to?' she asked, her voice low, almost threatening.

Kev tossed his bag in the corner of the kitchen. 'What?'

'Don't come the innocent with me. You've been at it again, haven't you?'

'What are you on about?' As the words left his mouth he heard a cough. A man's cough. It came from the living-room. 'Is that Dad? He's still alive then.' It had been a week since he'd seen Dad, seven days for the resentment to build up. But there was more than anger in his voice. There was hope too.

'It's not your dad,' said Mum, her voice still hard. 'It's your uncle Dave. He says you've been doing it again.' Mum's voice broke. She stubbed out her cigarette and immediately reached for another.

'Doing what?' Kev stared at her. He was genuinely bewildered. He'd been trying so hard to make her proud of him. Now it had all gone wrong and he didn't know why.

The ferocity had gone from Mum's voice. Instead there was anxiety. Disappointment too. 'The fires, love. You promised you would never do it again. You swore. Please tell me it isn't true.'

'That's easy,' said Kev, reeling from the barrage of questions. 'It isn't true. What's going on?'

'You tell me,' said Mum. 'Dave, will you come in here a sec?'

Dave appeared at the door. He looked serious. 'I didn't want to say anything, Kev lad. I was up half the night wondering what to do. But I had to tell Carol. It's only fair.'

Kev stared uncomprehendingly first at uncle Dave, then at Mum. He felt as if he was going mad. 'Tell her. Tell her what?'

'Oh, come on Kev,' said uncle Dave. 'Don't make this any more difficult than it already is.'

Kev slammed his fist down on the kitchen surface in frustration. 'Talk sense, will you?' he cried. 'I haven't got a clue what you're on about. First she starts on at me about the fires, then you ...' He pulled up short. 'You don't really think I'd start again?'

Uncle Dave rubbed at his chin. 'I was there, lad. I saw you.'

'Where?' demanded Kev. 'Where did you see me?'

'On the waste ground opposite the Community Centre.'

Kev couldn't believe it.

'Oh, come off it, Kev. Last night, about eight. I was

locking up after the Aerobics class. I saw the whole thing.'

'I was nowhere near there,' said Kev. 'I swear it ...' He found himself examining one of Gareth's drawings on the kitchen table. A dragon ... or was it a crocodile with wings? 'What time did you say?'

'Just after eight. Five, maybe ten past.'

'That's it then,' said Kev, seizing on his new information. 'I was round Bashir's. Jamie was there too. I came home from yours then went straight there. It's true. Ask them. Ask Mrs Gulaid. She was in.' He looked expectantly at Mum and uncle Dave. 'What am I supposed to have done anyway?'

'I can only tell you what I saw,' said uncle Dave. 'The trouble started when some teenagers turned up in a stolen car. I heard some shouting and looked up. Next thing I know it's on fire. That's when I saw you.'

'Me?' Kev repeated. He'd started laughing. He didn't quite know why, but he couldn't help it. The whole thing was just so stupid. 'But it couldn't be. What made you think it was me anyway?'

'That Everton shirt. The one you got for your birthday.'

'Behave,' Kev said dismissively. 'Half the lads on the estate have got them.' His stomach was churning. No way was Mum going to find out about his shirt.

Uncle Dave shook his head. 'Not with your name on the back, they haven't.'

Kev's eyes widened. His mind was racing. The whole thing was crazy, just crazy.

'That's right. It had McGovern plastered right across it. I thought it was daft at the time. Wearing a ski mask to cover your face and a shirt with your name on.'

'He had a mask?'

'What's this *he* nonsense?' said Dave irritably. 'Why

don't you have the decency to own up? You're only making it worse for yourself.'

Kev gave a strangled cry and struck his head with his fists. 'Why don't you listen?' he yelled. 'I was round Bashir's. I never went near South Road.'

Uncle Dave still looked unconvinced. Mum was more forgiving. 'You swear you weren't there?' she asked. 'I'll ask Mrs Gulaid, you know.'

'Ask her,' Kev interrupted. 'I want you to rotten well ask her.'

'You're really sticking to this story?' asked uncle Dave, his face registering doubt for the first time.

'I'm sticking to it,' said Kev, struggling to control himself, 'Because it's the truth.'

'I hope so,' said uncle Dave, 'Because those fire bobbies were hopping mad. It's a wonder Ronnie didn't say something at the game.'

'Ronnie?'

'That's right,' said uncle Dave. 'He was driving the fire engine. The moment the firefighters got out to tackle the blaze the lads started lobbing stones. One of the crew got a right crack in the face. She needed hospital treatment.'

'That's it then,' Kev murmured. 'That's why Ronnie's been freezing me out.'

Mum and uncle Dave exchanged glances. 'You promise me you weren't there?' asked Mum.

'Honest,' Kev replied. 'I never. I wouldn't let you down, Mum. Not again.'

'But what about the shirt?' Mum demanded immediately. 'How do you explain that?'

Kev hung his head. 'It's gone missing out of my locker.' There, said it.

'When?'

'A few days.'

He saw Mum's raised eyebrow.

'Honest.'

Mum seemed to be trying to make sense of Kev's story. For such a long time she just chewed at her nails, then she looked up. 'Dave, would you do me a favour?'

'Sure.'

'Mind Gareth for me. I'm going to check this story of Kev's with Mrs Gulaid.'

Kev shot to the door. 'I'll come with you.'

'No,' said Mum. 'I'd rather you stayed with Dave. I won't be a minute.'

As she slipped out Kev turned to uncle Dave. 'I'm telling the truth,' he said. 'Somebody's set me up.'

Uncle Dave filled the kettle to make a pot of tea. He had his back to Kev when he finally answered. 'I hope so, Kev. I really do hope so.'

Seven

About the same time that Sunday afternoon Chris was watching Gerwyn as he examined his school uniform.

'Try the blazer on again,' said Gerwyn, slipping it over Chris's shoulders.

'Lay off,' Chris protested, dumping the blazer on the floor. 'It'll do.'

Gerwyn's hands had only brushed him for a second but he hated it. He had no business fussing over the rotten blazer. Trying on your first High School uniform, getting ready for the seniors, they're things you do with your mum and dad, not a lousy social worker. Though it's a bit of a problem if they've cleared off on you.

'The sleeves are a bit long.'

'I said,' Chris snarled, 'They'll do.'

Gerwyn's touch had set something off in him. It reminded him that nobody had ever touched him. Not Dad and certainly not Mum. Nobody cared enough. He'd lived half his life without touching and that triggered his anger. Anger at his missing parents, anger at Gerwyn, anger at himself.

'Yes,' said Gerwyn attempting a joke. 'Like my mam said: You'll grow into it. You know what I used to say to her?'

'No,' Chris muttered, 'But I'm sure you're going to tell me.'

'When? I used to say. In the year 2000?'

'Bet she laughed at that,' said Chris, heavy on the sarcasm.

'She did actually,' said Gerwyn, nettled that his joke had belly-flopped.

Chris had noticed Gerwyn's voice beginning to falter after the mention of his mother. He was obviously wondering if he'd put his foot in it. Mothers weren't usually mentioned in front of Chris. He remembered the confusion on his teacher's face at primary school.

What could she do with that moody Power boy while the rest of the class were making Mother's Day cards? As it turned out she didn't need to worry. Chris let her off the hook by throwing a chair across the classroom and getting sent to sit outside the Headteacher's office. Better than stupid Mother's Day cards any day.

'Sounds like she had problems, your old lady,' observed Chris.

'Just one,' chuckled Gerwyn. 'Me.'

Chris decided to humour Gerwyn and slipped on the blazer after all. 'Why all the fuss anyway?' he asked. 'It's only rotten Scarisbrick. I'm not starting at Eton, you know.'

'It's still your first day at High School,' said Gerwyn. 'And where did you hear about Eton?'

'I'm not thick you know,' snapped Chris. In fact he'd always been one of the brightest boys in class at primary school. The problem was his temper. Just when he'd started to show what he was made of somebody would rub him up the wrong way. Then – whammo – the Head's office again. After a few doses of the old zero tolerance he just gave up trying.

'Whoa whoa,' said Gerwyn, holding up his hands. 'Did I call you stupid? It was just a bit unexpected, that's all.'

'I know lots of stuff like that,' Chris told him firmly. 'There's just one thing I don't know.'

'What's that?'

Why I'm on my own. But that isn't what he said. Just: 'Why they had to pick a uniform this colour.'

'Mm.' Gerwyn agreed. 'It is a bit grim, isn't it?'

'I mean,' Chris continued dolefully. 'Brown! I'll look like a Rollo with legs. Yeah, just look at me – Mars Bar on a stick.'

Gerwyn laughed. 'Now that's a picture I'll keep in my head.'

Chris found himself smiling back. It was hard not to let the barriers down with Gerwyn. He was a bit like a kid himself.

'Anyway, Chris,' said Gerwyn, the smile fading from his face. 'There is something else I wanted to mention.'

The old blankness returned to Chris's face. The barriers were back up. 'What's that?'

'I thought you'd be expecting it. It's Crusty. He says you hit him.'

'I never!'

'You do have a tendency ...'

'But I never!'

'He said you punched him in the ribs.'

'Liar!'

Chris was clenching his fists tight and drumming his heels against the base of the bed. 'He's just a lousy, stinking liar.'

'OK, OK,' said Gerwyn. 'You say it's not true.'

'It's not.'

'But we've talked about this before, haven't we?'

'Yeah,' sneered Chris. 'We do nothing but. Nag, nag, flipping nag. You do-gooders are all the same.'

'Listen,' said Gerwyn, passing over the do-gooder jibe. 'It might only be a couple of weeks until you move out. Don't you think you could try to get on with Crusty? Just till you leave.'

'Then tell him to keep his thieving hands off my stuff.'

'I did,' said Gerwyn.

'Because next time,' said Chris, 'I'll cut his rotten hands off.'

'I told him,' said Gerwyn, ignoring Chris's threat. 'He says he'll keep to his own side of the room.'

'Sure,' said Chris, 'And he always sticks by his promises, doesn't he?'

'I know he gets on your nerves, Chris,' said Gerwyn. 'But lots of people are going to do that. At Scarisbrick, for example. You can't punch all their lights out, now can you?'

'If they touch my stuff I will,' said Chris stubbornly.

'And if they're bigger than you?'

'There are ways,' Chris replied. 'The bigger they come ...'

'Yes, I know, the harder they fall. All I'm saying is, keep a rein on that temper. Try counting to ten.'

'You're sure I won't get stuck halfway?' Chris retorted.

'Now that's not fair,' said Gerwyn. 'You just took me the wrong way. I never said you were thick.'

Chris remembered Mrs Carrick's class and all the time he spent on her naughty table. 'You're about the only one who hasn't.'

'Yes maybe,' said Gerwyn. 'But you've got a new start at Scarisbrick tomorrow. And another with the Taskers. Try to make it work, eh?' With that Gerwyn left the room and made his way downstairs. For a few moments Chris looked after him. New start, he thought, who was Gerwyn kidding? Kids like me don't get new starts. Then, walking across the room, he picked up Crusty's Game Boy.

'Snitch on me, did you?' he said aloud. 'Well, this is what you get.' He tossed the Game Boy from hand to hand, then without another word he shoved open the window and dropped it into the garden.

Eight

It's Costello. It's got to be. I've been turning it over every which way, and it always comes out the same. Costello and Brain Damage must have gone in our changing rooms and nicked my shirt. Revenge for beating them three–one in the second game of the season. Of course it's them. Who else would want to put me in the frame? It takes single-minded sheer rottenness to do a thing like that. Dirty thieving toe-rags! They've dropped me right in it. Mum's fuming over my shirt. As if that isn't bad enough, she's still not sure I haven't been getting up to something. Mrs Gulaid wasn't much help. She said she was busy with the baby. She couldn't be sure what time I left. Bashir could, but Mum wasn't prepared to listen to him. Reckons he'd give me an alibi even if I'd just bombed Disneyworld. Well, I'm not taking this lying down. You wait till tomorrow. I'm going to have it out with the poison pair. I'll drag them both in front of Ronnie if I have to. Nobody's going to make a monkey out of me. Mum wants me to be on my best behaviour for my first day at Scarisbrick, especially after this stuff with the fire brigade. Fair enough. I will be. In school, that is. But she never said anything about outside. Which is where I'm going to have it out with them. This feud's been going on for a year now ever since I put Brain Damage's nose out of joint by showing him up in front of his mates. But if Costello and Brain Damage think they can sink me with a lousy trick like this they've got another think coming. It's Kev McGovern they're dealing with, the Guv'nor. No matter what it takes, I'm getting my shirt back. And clearing my name with Mum. Ronnie too. You've been warned Brain Damage. And you Costello, I'm coming to get you.

Nine

Kev was first off the bus, earning himself a disapproving glare from the middle-aged man he'd brushed aside in his haste to intercept Brain Damage and Costello.

'Are you sure it was them, Guv?' asked Jamie, following him off the bus.

'Of course I'm sure.'

'So where are they?'

Kev squinted against the stinging September wind as he searched among the brown-blazered tide streaming into the gates of Scarisbrick High. 'Dunno. Rats, I've lost them. Stupid flaming bus driver. He could have let us off at those lights like I asked.' Jamie rolled his eyes.

He hadn't exactly jumped at the chance of an early confrontation with Brain Damage and Costello. Mum would kill him if he got into trouble on his first day at secondary school.

'Just when I thought I had them,' snarled Kev. 'Come on, Jay, we'll catch them later.' Jamie gave a sigh of relief. He was nervous enough about starting his new school without having to worry about Kev dragging him into a fight.

'What if they don't admit to it?' Jamie asked. 'You can't make them?'

'Who can't?'

Jamie grimaced. There was no talking to Kev when he was in this mood. He looked across the dual carriageway at the school gates and his stomach clenched. 'You nervous, Guv?'

'What?' Kev was still preoccupied with spotting Costello and Brain Damage. 'Oh, nervous. Of course not. Just another stupid school, isn't it? Same old story, same old lies.'

'Yes, s'pose so.'

'Guv! Jamie!' They looked up to see Daz, Joey and Jimmy waving from just inside the gates. 'Hurry up, you'll be late for induction.'

'Induction?' Kev repeated, giving Jamie an enquiring look. 'What the heck's that?'

'Didn't you read that letter we got?' Jamie asked.

'Nah. Binned it before Mum could get her hands on it. What did it say?'

'We go in the hall. All us Year Sevens. To meet our teachers.'

'That should be thrilling,' Kev yawned.

Jamie smiled indulgently. Same old Guv.

'So Costello and Brain Damage will be there?' Kev asked.

Jamie stopped. 'Oh, you're not going to kick off, are you?'

Kev shook his head. 'I can't. Promised Mum, didn't I? I want to let them know I've got my eye on them, that's all.'

'Promise you won't have a go at them?' Jamie asked anxiously. 'Because if you start something I'm not going to sit by you.'

'Keep your lid on,' said Kev. 'Nothing's going to happen in school.'

'You sure about that?'

'Positive,' Kev insisted. 'I promised Mum, and I'd never go back on my word to her. She's stuck by me through the bad times. I owe her.'

'Right, then I'll sit with you.' Jamie quickened his pace and started to cross the road. 'Daz, Jimmy, Joey, hang on for us.'

As the Scarisbrick Head Mr Croft welcomed the boys to their new school Kev sat making little tears round the edge of the handout he'd been given. His indifference was in sharp contrast to the interest shown by his mates. He was too obsessed with the frame-up to listen. He'd asked Jimmy if Ronnie had said anything to him, but Jimmy didn't know anything.

'So,' Mr Croft concluded. 'Your form teachers will call your names and you will be taken to class. Mrs Spinks,' He indicated a short, dark-haired woman to his left, 'Would you like to call the names of your form?'

Kev had finally located Costello and Brain Damage two rows behind and was glaring at them when Jamie nudged him in the ribs.

'Huh? What's up?'

'It's us,' said Jamie excitedly. 'We're in the same form. That's good, isn't it?'

'Yes, sure.'

'See you, lads,' said Jamie. 'Hope you get somebody decent.' His fellow-Diamonds nodded.

'Just us then, is it?' asked Kev. 'Nobody we know in with us?'

'Ratso's with us.'

Ratso grinned. He was relieved. His best mate Gord had got in at the Bluecoat, so he'd been worried about being on his own. Kev smiled back. While you've got Diamonds you've got friends.

'Brain Damage and Costello have got that big, lanky feller. Mr Graham, I think he's called. They're in with your Cheryl.'

'Poor Cheryl,' said Kev. He was about to add a comment when he registered a familiar face just in front of him. 'It's Chris, isn't it?' he asked.

'Yes, what's it to you?' said Chris turning hostile eyes Kev's way. 'Do I know you?'

'I saw you on Saturday,' said Kev. 'You're moving into our Cheryl's, aren't you?'

The same frosty reception. 'Am I?'

'That's what uncle Dave and aunty Pat said.'

'Must be true then.' And that was it. Without another word Chris turned and followed Mrs Spinks to class.

'Friendly sort, isn't he?' said Jamie.

'Not half,' said Kev. 'Real little charmer. Snake charmer, that is.'

'So how come he's moving into Cheryl's?'

'It's uncle Dave and aunty Pat,' Kev explained. 'They've got into fostering.'

'Yes?' said Ratso. 'Rather them than me. I don't like the look of him, myself.'

'Can't judge a book by its cover,' said Jamie.

Kev laughed. 'Where'd you come up with that, Jay?'

Jamie blushed. 'It means ...'

'Yes, yes,' said Kev. 'I know what it means.'

It was at that moment that Mrs Spinks clapped her hands and called for quiet. She told them they were Class 7S. That's S for Spinks. S for Stinks more like, thought Kev, entering the classroom and taking in his new surroundings. He glanced at Chris, but Chris looked right through him. First Ronnie, now Chris. All of a sudden everybody seemed to be cutting him dead.

Ten

Chris looked up. That nosy kid again. The one who said he was related to the Taskers. He was making a bee-line towards him across the yard. It was the way Chris had always been; he was actually scared of making friends. In case *they* let him down too. Just like Mum and Dad and everybody else in his life.

He eyed Kev and his mates suspiciously. What were they after anyway? 'What's with you, why can't you leave me alone?'

'We're only trying to be friendly,' said Kev. 'Seeing as you're almost family.'

'Meaning?'

'Well,' Kev explained. 'You'll be living at my uncle and aunty's so ...'

'So nothing,' Chris retorted acidly. 'That doesn't make me family. Just makes me a rotten parcel to be passed around.'

'What *is* your problem?' asked Kev, starting to lose patience.

Now Chris was arguing back for the sake of it. To show he was tough. To show he didn't need Mr Nosy. Or anybody else for that matter. My problem? thought Chris. 'At the moment ... *you*.'

Jamie and Ratso turned towards Kev. Just how was the Guv'nor going to react to that?

'Come on, lads,' said Kev, clearly stung by the reply. 'There's no helping some people.'

'Help?' snorted Chris. 'What makes you think I need your help?'

'I just thought ...' Kev's voice trailed off.

'You thought you'd stick your nose in,' Chris interrupted. 'Just like your do-gooding relatives.'

Kev's face registered utter bewilderment at Chris's attitude. Nobody, but nobody, spoke to him that way.

'There's no need to be like that,' said Ratso, giving Kev some unsolicited help.

Chris's features twisted angrily. Oh, and you'd know, would you?

'And you can butt out,' snapped Chris. 'I don't need anybody. Got that?'

'Forget it, lads,' said Jamie. 'He's off his head.'

The words were only half out of Jamie's mouth when Chris pushed himself away from the wall he'd been leaning on. *Off my head! Off my head for hating this stupid rotten life!* Seizing Jamie by the lapels of his new blazer, Chris swung him round.

'Gerroff!'

'Take that back, you ming!'

'Get off me.'

Chris slammed Jamie against the wall. Like he was dealing with everything that had ever hurt him. He'd swung Jamie hard. Hard enough to wind him. 'Say sorry,' he demanded. 'Nobody talks to me that way.'

Jamie was wriggling in vain to break Chris's grip.

'I didn't mean anything,' he said, deciding to backtrack. 'I just meant you were acting a bit off.'

Kev tried to intervene. 'Cool it eh, Chris' he said gently. 'Nobody meant anything. You've got us all wrong.'

Chris bounced Jamie back against the wall and turned on Kev. 'What's with you?' he barked. 'No good at taking a hint, are you? I want you and your stupid mates to get out of my face.'

Kev, Jamie and Ratso might have done just that, but Costello and Brain Damage arrived right on cue. They'd been watching the altercation from a distance and obviously thought they could turn it to their advantage. 'This bunch bothering you?' Costello asked Chris.

'Clear off,' warned Jamie. 'This is nothing to do with you, rat face.'

'That's for him to say,' Costello shot back. 'Need some help?'

'No,' Chris replied. 'I fight my own battles.' He was confused. First Mr Nosy, now some rotten carrot top. Suddenly, everybody was after him. What did this lot want?

It was Brain Damage's turn to join in. 'You've got to admit, you're a bit outnumbered. We're on your side. What's your name, anyway?'

'That's my business,' Chris told him. He was aware of even more kids arriving, taking sides without knowing what the whole thing was about. And that kid had called *him* crazy! Everything was spinning out of control. He felt like somebody had put a vice on his head and was tightening it. Slowly.

'Got trouble, Guv?' asked one.

'It's OK, John,' said Kev. 'I can handle it.'

'You reckon, McGovern?' sneered Costello. 'Look around you.'

Up to fifteen boys had descended on Chris, jostling and shoving. They were using him, making him an excuse for their own stupid little battles. Well, they could find another fall guy. The vice was still tightening, crushing him, making the veins in his temple bulge.

'I'm not looking at anyone but you, Costello,' Kev replied. 'While you're here I think you've got something of mine.'

Chris wasn't even listening to the quarrel any more. He was choking on his own frustration and anger.

'Like what?' asked Costello.

'Like my Everton shirt, the one with my name on.'

To Jamie's horror, Kev seized the sleeve of Costello's blazer. *But you promised.*

'And,' said Kev, 'I want it back.'

'Take your hands off me,' said Costello.

'Or,' Brain Damage added, 'You'll regret it.'

'Yeah?' Kev murmured. 'So who's going to make me?'

Chris's head was splitting, the voices of the crowd around him magnified enormously. They were using him, all of them. Like always. Everybody was just out for themselves. Nobody cared about him, about what he wanted. Suddenly his blood was pulsing like molten lava. He clenched his fists and went for the nearest of the surrounding boys.

'What the ... ?'

Costello was the victim of Chris's random onslaught. The rest of the crowd looked on in astonishment as Chris laid into him with both fists.

'Fight,' shouted a couple of boys on the edge of the action. The refrain was taken up by others. 'Fight, fight, fight.' Then by knots of boys rushing over to get a grandstand view. 'Fight, fight, *fight*.'

But Costello wasn't doing much fighting. Chris was lashing out with hands and feet, the sheer frenzy of his attack crushing any hope of defence.

'Watch out,' hissed Ratso. 'Teacher coming.' The crowd started to melt away, but Chris wasn't even aware of the teacher's approach. He cuffed Costello repeatedly across the head as he sank to his knees.

'Break it up!' yelled the teacher on duty. 'I said: break it up.'

Chris at last came to his senses. He stared down at the subdued and bloodied Costello as if to say: *How did he get down there?*

'Come with me,' said the teacher. 'Both of you.' As Chris and Costello were marched away Cheryl arrived at Kev's side.

'Is that who I think it is?' she asked.

'It's Chris.'

'Great,' Cheryl groaned. 'And this is the kid Mum and Dad want to have living with us.'

'That's some temper he's got,' Jamie observed.

'I'm just glad he directed it at Costello,' said Ratso. 'And not at me.'

'Yes,' said Kev, thoughtfully rubbing his chin, 'Looks like he's got the hump with the gang. Now we've got to see if we can keep it that way.'

'How do you mean, Guv?'

'Simple,' said Kev. 'I'd rather have him on our side than theirs.'

Jamie was still sore from Chris's rough handling. 'Amen to that,' he said. 'Amen to that.'

Eleven

Kev was found that Monday evening kicking his heels outside South Road Community Centre. For once he'd made his excuses to Jamie and Bashir. He wouldn't be walking up with them. He'd see them there. Something to do. He had to be early to catch Ronnie. And he had to see him on his own. Some things are best done without an audience. 'Come on, Ron,' he said out loud. He looked up the road. No sign of Ronnie's black Carlton. Instead he saw somebody he could have done with avoiding. Uncle Dave on his way to open up the Community Centre.

'Hi there, Kev,' he said. 'You're early. I thought training didn't start till half past.'

'It doesn't,' said Kev. 'I came early to see someone.'

'Not that Helen, is it? Still a bit young for the ladies, aren't you?'

Kev frowned. 'No, not Helen.' He was feeling uncomfortable. Did Dave know about events in school that dinner time?

'I've just been on the phone to your mum,' said Dave. He sounded cheerful. Which meant he probably hadn't heard about Chris.

'Yes?' said Kev. 'What about?'

'You.'

Kev's heart skipped. 'How come?'

'I was just telling her I thought we'd jumped to conclusions. She agreed. That's right,' said Dave, smiling at the look of surprise on Kev's face. 'We believe you.'

'You do?'

'We always *wanted* to. Especially Carol. I know she's

hard on you, but she loves the bones of you, Kev. You've got to admit it looked pretty bad.'

'Sure,' said Kev, still smarting from the injustice. 'Whatever.'

'Friends eh?' said Dave, offering his hand.

Kev took it and they shook self-consciously.

'You do believe me then?'

'You're a changed kid these last twelve months,' said Dave. 'I can't believe you'd let yourself down.'

'Thanks, uncle Dave.'

They both turned at the sound of tyres crunching on gravel. It was Ronnie.

'This who you were waiting for?' asked Dave.

'Uh huh, I just hope *he* believes me.'

'Do you want me to have a word with him?'

'Thanks,' said Kev, watching Ronnie locking and alarming the car. 'But no thanks. This is down to me.'

Dave gave Ronnie a wave and left them to it.

'Not got your crew with you this evening?' asked Ronnie, hauling a bag of footballs out of the boot.

'No. I wanted to catch you on your own.'

Ronnie's eyes squinted to a thin line. 'Why, have you got something to tell me?'

'Yes, but it isn't what you're thinking.'

Ronnie shoved his car keys into his jacket pocket. 'And what am I thinking?'

'That I had something to do with that robbed car.'

'Didn't you?'

Kev wanted to protest his innocence but he kept a rein on his emotions. 'No, and I didn't chuck any stones either.'

'I'm glad to hear it.'

Ronnie started to walk towards the practice ground.

'Hang on,' said Kev. 'Don't you want to hear the rest?'

'If you say you didn't do it,' Ronnie told him, 'Then you didn't do it.'

Kev found himself calling after the manager. 'I didn't. Somebody nicked my shirt. I think I know who.'

'Those lads from the Liver Bird?' Ronnie suggested. 'Ramage and Costello.'

Kev was taken aback. 'How did you know?'

Ronnie unfastened the bag of size-four footballs. 'Jamie and Bashir called on me,' he said. 'They've already put your side. You've got friends, Kevin. Good friends.'

Kev felt his eyes stinging. 'I know,' he said. 'They're the best. Just the best.'

'Here,' said Ronnie. 'That's the key to the stock cupboard in the Community Centre. Bring the nets. We can have them up by the time the rest of the lads arrive.'

Kev glanced down at the key. He knew it was a gesture of trust. 'You thought it was me though, didn't you?'

'I'm no saint,' said Ronnie. 'My mates get bricked by somebody wearing your shirt. What am I supposed to think?'

'So why didn't you say anything to me? Why just ignore me?'

'I was hoping you'd own up,' explained Ronnie. 'I respect somebody who's got the guts to admit to their mistakes. Now it looks like there's nothing to explain.'

'There isn't,' said Kev. 'I'll fetch the nets.' As he jogged towards the Community Centre Ronnie called after him.

'One thing you've got to promise me, Kev.'

'What's that?'

'No getting your own back on those two.'

'You've got my word.' And if you believe that, Kev thought, you'll believe anything.

Twelve

It was a breezy, sunlit Tuesday morning. Almost a happy one, Chris thought. For starters, he'd got away with a caution after that fight in school. A disruption slip, it was called. Now he could look forward to his second day at Scarisbrick. If you ever look forward to school, that is. On the way to the Head of Year he'd actually been worried what Gerwyn would say. Not that he was scared or anything. But he didn't see any point disappointing him for the sake of it. Though he would never say so to his face, Gerwyn had always been decent to him. Decent for a do-gooder, that is. A voice made him start.

'Everything go all right yesterday?' Talk of the devil. It was Gerwyn coming through the front door. He hadn't been on duty when Chris got back from school so they hadn't spoken yet.

'Yes, fine.'

'You didn't wreck the place then? You didn't nail any of the teachers' heads to the floor?'

'No, it was OK.' Which was a weird thing to say after everything that had happened. Even weirder, he really meant it. He'd shown that he wasn't a kid to be messed with.

'OK,' mimicked Gerwyn in his most unenthusiastic voice. 'That all?'

'All right,' said Chris, 'So it was fantabulous.' Heavy on the irony.

'No need to go over the top.'

'As the circus master said to the acrobatic elephant,' quipped Chris.

Gerwyn's face registered surprise. Chris was actually sounding cheerful. 'Careful Chris,' said Gerwyn. 'You might even smile.'

'You never know,' said Chris.

'Has something happened?'

Chris handed Gerwyn the letter that had arrived that morning. 'Great,' said Gerwyn, running his eyes over it. 'You've got a moving-in date with the Taskers. Excited?'

'Of course not.' But he was. Until he actually saw it in black and white he hadn't really believed it was going to happen. Suddenly his life was changing, and so quickly it made him dizzy, like he was on top of a fairground ride and the down-slope was masked by fog. Maybe things wouldn't be so bad after all. Maybe he could even have a half-normal life. What with the lucky escape at school and the impromptu party the other kids had thrown for him at breakfast time he was feeling as close to good as he could remember. Not that he was about to let it show. That would be weakness.

'What about Crusty?' Chris must have looked puzzled. 'Have you said sorry for hitting him yet?' Crusty had been the one who turned breakfast into a party.

'We're getting on fine,' Chris told Gerwyn. He was feeling guilty. Well, almost.

Gerwyn smiled. It was as much as he could expect. He glanced at his watch. 'You'd better hurry up,' he said. 'It's twenty-to-nine already.'

'I'm gone,' said Chris. As he closed the door behind him he looked back at the home. He soon would be.

Within five minutes Chris suddenly remembered the

problem with feeling good about the world – there were other people there and at least half of them had it in for him. He was taking a short cut through the Health Centre car park when he realized he was being followed. The red-headed kid from the day before. What was his name? Yes, Costello, that's what the Head of Year called him. He had at least three of his mates with him. Chris quickened his pace. He was within sprinting distance of the school gates. No sense hanging around inviting trouble. He was about to make a break for it when one of the gang sprinted ahead to block his way.

'Like to finish what you started yesterday?' came the challenge. 'With me.'

Chris hesitated. Not with four other kids waiting to join in.

'What's up?' the boy asked. 'Know my reputation, do you?'

Chris's mind was working overtime trying to come up with a plan. Unfortunately, his mouth was quicker off the blocks than his brain. 'I can guess,' he said. 'You're the one they call Brain Damage, aren't you?'

'The name,' growled Brain Damage, 'Is Ramage. Andy Ramage.' Ramage? Why did that ring a bell?

'Well, Andy Ramage,' said Chris, still puzzling over the name, 'I'm asking you to get out of my way.'

'Hear that, Andy,' chortled Costello. 'He's asking you?'

'Say please,' Brain Damage ordered.

Chris felt the anger rising. If there was one thing he remembered about his dad it was his advice. *You never give way to any man.* Good, bad or indifferent, it was a piece of advice that stuck in his mind. 'You,' he told Costello, 'Had better back off. Or do you want another black eye to add to the one I gave you yesterday?'

Costello touched his left eye self-consciously. To be taken that easily had been humiliating.

'As for you,' he said, turning on Brain Damage, 'What happened between me and him is none of your business.'

'Oh, isn't it?' said Brain Damage. 'Well, we'll see about that.'

Chris watched him coming forward. That's when he got a hook on the name. Ramage. That's right – Lee Ramage. How could he have forgotten? The guy who was responsible for his dad ending up in Walton nick. 'Have you got a brother?' Chris demanded, stopping Brain Damage in his tracks.

'Yes, two,' Brain Damage answered. 'What of it?'

Chris's eyes turned hard and cold. 'Lee. Is one of them called Lee?' Chris remembered what Dad had told him before his arrest. *Ramage has come on my turf for the last time. I'm going to sort him.* Only it was Dad who got sorted. Good style. Dad had arrived tooled up at Ramage's flat only to find the police waiting for him. Had to go and deck one, didn't he? And with a baseball bat, too. If there's a direct route to prison, it's doing a copper. *Go straight to jail, do not collect 200 pounds.*

'That's right. Our kid is Lee Ramage. What of it?'

That had been the crunch, his dad going down. Mum was already long gone by then, but he still had Dad. He still had somebody to hang onto in this crazy world. Until Ramage came along.

'Get on your knees and beg,' said Brain Damage, 'And I might only knock half your teeth out.'

'Let's see it then, moron,' Costello added. 'I want to see you grovel.' Their mates roared with laughter. They were loving every minute of it.

'What did you call me?' Chris asked in a low voice. *You never give way to any man.*

'Moron,' Costello informed. 'Why, want to make something of it, *moron*?'

Never give way. Especially to Lee Ramage's brother. Chris didn't say a word. He just flung himself at Brain Damage. Taken unawares, the taller boy staggered back. Costello joined the fray, kicking and punching. Chris retaliated, winding him, only to find himself facing three more opponents.

'Come on, Carl,' said one. 'Let's have him.'

Chris didn't care about the others. It was Brain Damage he wanted. Shoving the one called Carl off balance he renewed his onslaught. This time Brain Damage was ready. As a pair of hands came from behind to cover his face, Chris felt a fist punching low and hard into his stomach. That first telling hit was the signal for a flurry of blows to rain down on his head, back and shoulders. Unable to see, he lashed out blindly.

'He's mad,' came a voice.

'Just get hold of his arms,' panted Costello. 'Pin him.'

Chris struggled but they had him. Two, maybe three pairs of hands were pinning his arms behind his back. Then a foot was hooked round his ankles. They were going to force him to the floor. His efforts to break free grew more desperate, but to no avail.

'That's it, Tez,' urged Brain Damage. 'Use your weight.'

Chris felt his knees buckle. He'd had it.

'Hey, Brain Damage, that's enough. *Enough*!'

Chris jerked his head. This was a new voice, but familiar somehow.

'Keep your nose out McGovern.'

Chris seized on the name. Him again, Cheryl's

cousin. What was he doing here? After everything he'd called him.

'Hear that?' chuckled Kev. 'Suddenly everybody's calling me nosy.'

Then all hell let loose around Chris. Shouts, cries, a kick in the kidneys and suddenly he could see. Costello and Brain Damage were edging away, and their gang with them.

'OK,' said Costello, 'So you've got us outnumbered. But this isn't over.'

'Oh, go play with your Barbies, Costello,' sneered Kev before turning his attention to Chris.

'You all right?'

Chris was shaky, but he wasn't about to let on. 'I'm fine.'

'Glad to hear it.' With that Kev and his mates turned towards school. Chris watched them for a few moments then he felt the urge to call them back. It was like somebody was pushing him forward, telling him not to miss the opportunity.

'Hang on,' said Chris, rising to his feet.

'What? I thought you didn't want to know us.'

Don't blow it, Chris told himself. Talk to them. 'Yeah, sorry about yesterday.'

'Apology accepted,' said Kev. 'Any enemy of Costello is a friend of mine.'

Chris's heart leapt. Friend! 'You don't hold it against me then?' he asked. 'The way I spoke to you.'

'That depends,' said Kev.

'On what?'

'On whether you're interested in football. Do you play?'

'Play?' Chris repeated, as if appalled at the idea that anybody didn't. 'Of course I play.'

'And who do you support?'

'Everton. I grew up sucking on a blue and white dummy.'

'Then,' said Kev, displaying the Everton badge on his jacket. 'This could be the start of a beautiful friendship.'

PART TWO

The Spark

One

At least the Diamonds are going OK. It almost makes up for the way Costello and Brain Damage set me up. You wait, you morons, I'll have you. So help me, I will. And you're not getting away with my shirt either. Anyway, keep your anger on ice, Kev lad. You'll get your chance. Right now the team's the thing. After starting the season with a squad so threadbare we could hardly field a full side, suddenly we've got three subs on the bench. OK, so Dougie Long's no Ronaldo but Liam Savage looks a good find, even if Conor does overshadow him a bit. As for Chris, he can move the ball about a bit. You should have seen him training. He even put a smile on Ronnie's face. I tell you, we're building strength in depth.

It couldn't come at a better time, either. Ratso's been going over the table and he tells me things could get interesting. Northend United slipped up last week against Sefton Dynamoes. They could only scrape a one–one draw. If they fail to win today and we beat St Bede's we'll move ahead of Northend into third place behind Ajax Aintree and Longmoor Celtic, the only sides who've still got a 100 per cent record. Then there's the mouth-watering prospect of meeting Ajax in a fortnight. After an opening day defeat against Longmoor we're actually within striking distance of the top spot. I'm just keeping my fingers crossed that nothing goes wrong. Let's face it, it usually does. I get these fits of panic sometimes, especially when I see that look on Chris's face. The old tick-a-tick timebomb look. He's like a dormant volcano, that one. Not that I can blame him. I mean, I always thought I was hard done by, but at least I've got Mum and Gareth and that's a family in my book.

Chris has nobody. I can't imagine it's much fun in that kid's home. Well, nothing's really your own, is it? And it's not like you choose who you're living with either.

His room-mate sounds a right weirdo. Sharing like that, he can't even shut him out. That must be awful. That's one thing about ours. My room is my sanctuary. No Gareth, no snooty Cheryl. Even Mum knocks before she comes in. Chris is worse off than me in the dad department too. He's got one somewhere, at least I think he has, but he doesn't seem to be part of his life at all. Mine's no great shakes, but at least he's around. Well, sort of. No, I wouldn't swop my life for Chris's, not for all the tea in China. I never thought I'd say this, but you know something, Kev McGovern, you're a lucky guy.

Two

Next Sunday morning Kev was having a rethink. He sank to his knees, clutching his head. 'Not again!' Conor's eighteen-yard drive had shaved the post and gone out for a goal kick. It was the third time they'd gone close within the first five minutes. Chris gave a sympathetic look from the subs bench. Kev registered it and turned to Conor.

'Hard luck, Con,' he said as he picked himself up.

'Pure bad luck,' said Conor. 'But it just wouldn't drop for me.' Just like Conor, thought Kev. It couldn't be that he just missed it, could it? There was no time to analyse the flight of the ball any further. Gord had already won the ball back for the Diamonds and had threaded it through to John.

'My ball,' shouted Kev and Conor together.

John chose Kev. With the ball at his feet, Kev slipped

his marker and dribbled infield. In the corner of his eye he glimpsed Bashir sprinting down the touch line. Brushing aside a challenge from a St Bede's defender, he rolled the ball into his path.

'Run it, Bash.' The Diamonds' winger took the ball in his stride, pushed it to the dead-ball line and screwed it back. It was a nightmare to defend.

'Clear it!' bawled Ewan Green, the big St Bede's centreback. But it was easier said than done. The cross evaded everybody, scudding through the area to the feet of John O'Hara for the Diamonds. He shot first time but sliced it. Fortunately for him, the St Bede's keeper was on hand to spare his blushes. He misjudged it completely and parried the ball when it was plainly going out for a goal kick. Conor was on hand to slot it home from close range.

One–nil.

'Peach,' he announced. 'How many goals have you got so far this season, Jamie?'

'Five,' Jamie replied.

'I've got four,' said Conor, giving him a wink. 'One behind you. Not for long, though.'

Jamie watched as he walked away. 'Arrogant beggar,' he said to Kev.

'Tell me about it,' said Kev. 'You've go to admit it, though. He's good.'

'He's not getting one over on me,' said Jamie.

'So what are you going to do about it?' asked Kev pointedly.

'Score, of course.'

'That's what I like to hear,' said Kev. 'Nothing like a bit of healthy competition to spice things up.'

Competition was right. For the next ten minutes the Diamonds' forwards were peppering the opposition goal with shots, Jamie and Conor vying with each other for the next goal. After a particularly speculative shot from all of twenty-five yards, Kev approached Jamie.

'Come on, Jay,' he grumbled. 'I was completely clear then. There is such a thing as teamwork you know.'

Jamie scowled at Conor. 'Tell him that,' he said. 'He never gives me the ball.'

Kev sighed. The competition didn't quite seem so healthy any more. 'I'll try.'

Midway through the first half all the Diamonds' pressure paid off. Ratso looked up and invited Kev to run on to his long, low pass. Nutmegging the oncoming defender, Kev drove into the penalty area and lined himself up for a shot. With the keeper and Ewan Green closing him down, there was no time to place the ball. He just swung at it. More by luck than good management, the shot was a screamer. The keeper did well to tip it over the bar.

'Hard luck,' Chris shouted encouragingly from the sidelines.

'OK lads,' Kev shouted. 'We haven't capitalized on our corners. Let's put this one in the back of the net.' But Jimmy Mintoe's kick was too long.

'Straight out of play,' grumbled Conor, giving up the chase. Nobody had told Bashir it was irretrievable, however. He pursued it to the line, stuck out a leg, turned and put it back into the danger area where Jamie was waiting to score with a half-volley.

'Brilliant strike!' yelled Chris. 'That's two–nil.' But there was another score Jamie was even more interested in at that moment.

'Six–four to me,' he told Conor. 'Still think you'll end up top scorer?'

'Piece of cake,' said Conor. 'Just watch me.'

'Listen to him, will you?' gasped Jamie. 'Head the

size of a rotten pumpkin.' The score at half-time remained two–nil.

'A two-goal cushion,' said Kev. 'That should keep Ronnie happy.' It didn't.

'What do you think you're playing at?' he demanded. 'You must have had sixty per cent possession out there, and what did you do with it?' He picked out Conor and Jamie. 'OK,' he continued, 'So you scored a couple. Big deal. If you'd been a bit less selfish and given the ball to players better placed to score we could have been four or five goals up. That's right, we could have put the game beyond them. As it is, they could still get back into it.'

'More like the old Ronnie,' Kev whispered to Jamie.

'So,' said Ronnie, punching home the point. 'Let's worry a bit less about ourselves as individuals and a bit more about the whole team.'

'No way, José,' said Conor, loudly enough to be heard.

Ronnie gave him a glare that would have cut any normal kid to the quick.

'Well?' said Conor. 'What's the big deal? We just need more of the same. We're walking it.'

'Don't listen to him,' said Chris as the team talk broke up. He'd been reluctant to join in the discussion earlier. He was only a sub, and a newcomer to boot. 'Ronnie's right. The Diamonds should have killed the game off in the first half. You could live to regret it.'

'*We* could live to regret it,' said Kev. 'You're one of us now, remember.'

'Oh yes,' said Chris. 'Sorry, I forgot.' He was finding it hard to believe he was actually part of something.

'And by the way,' said Kev. 'For once, I'm with Conor. We've got this bunch just where we want them.

We're fire-proof.' But Kev was wrong. Ten minutes into the second half St Bede's wingback Sean Laker beat Joey Bannen for pace and crossed it for their tall centreforward Brian Dinsdale to head home. The goal had Daz beating the ground in frustration.

'What was that?' he roared at his defenders. 'He caught you completely flat-footed. Why didn't anybody pick him up?' Five minutes later it got even worse. Dinsdale was the tormentor again, trapping the ball on the penalty spot and netting it coolly.

'For crying out loud!' said Kev. 'They're back on terms. Come on, lads, we've got to break up their rhythm. Get in tight. Don't give them any time on the ball.' The Diamonds tightened up their act but it didn't stop Dinsdale giving them a few more frights. Exploiting a slip by Ant Glover on the edge of the area the St Bede's striker went one on one with Daz. This time it was the big Diamonds' keeper who came off best, pushing the shot on to the post and back into play.

'Right,' said Kev, 'That was their chance to take the lead. Don't give them another.'

As both sides tired, play was suddenly stretched with spaces opening up all over the field. It was a tailor-made situation for Bashir. Picking up the ball on the halfway line he went through the St Bede's defence like a hot wire through plastic. The Diamonds' forwards made their runs, Jamie to the near post, Conor to the far. In the event, Bashir chose neither. Kev was flying into the box unmarked. Bashir held off his marker then squeezed between him and the goal line, flicking the ball towards his skipper. Kev dived just at the right moment and headed the ball into the top left-hand corner.

'Goal!'

St Bede's came back at them in the last five minutes and they had the Diamonds rocking. It was only Daz's cat-like reflexes that stopped them levelling the score.

'Think you can keep them out?' Ronnie asked, turning to his subs.

'You talking to me?' asked Chris.

'You and Liam,' Ronnie answered. 'I want to hold on to this lead. That last run finished Bashir and Ratso isn't doing much.'

'What about me?' asked Dougie.

'Not today, son,' said Ronnie. With that, he made his substitutions.

'No fancy stuff,' said Kev, hands on knees. 'The lads are out on their feet. If it comes near you, just launch it.'

Twice crosses from the dead-ball line threw the Diamonds into a panic and twice Chris was on hand to head the ball powerfully out.

'That's it,' said Kev approvingly. 'Just get it clear.' On the stroke of full time, as the ref lifted the whistle to his mouth, Brian Dinsdale had Diamonds' hearts skipping a beat for the last time. Running on to a mistimed defensive header by Gord, he volleyed the ball back at goal. It was a terrific strike. Left unsighted by the crowd of players in front of him, Daz was well beaten. But not Chris. He'd planted himself on the goal line and was on hand to smash the ball to safety. As Ewan Green raced to fetch it, the whistle blew.

'Brilliant,' cried a jubilant Kev McGovern. 'Me, Conor and Jamie got the goals, but it was that clearance that got us all three points. Welcome to the Diamonds, Chris.'

Chris was smiling. Not just with his lips, but with his whole body. It felt like he'd come home.

Three

That win over St Bede's was a turning point. I can feel it. On the first day of the season we were struggling to field a side and went down to defeat. Just a month later we're breathing down the necks of the front-runners and suddenly we're feeling invincible. Conor was awesome and Chris did a lot to banish any doubts I had. Seems a team player to me. Then there's the little bonus of Brain Damage getting sent off in their game against Warbreck. That's right, violent conduct. Ratso told us after the match. It'll mean a two-match suspension, and about time. The Liver Birds are going to have some disciplinary record. They've had three dismissed already this season. It's not just on the field that things are picking up either. Bashir says Lee Ramage is leaving the shop alone. He must have got the message. The place belongs to Mr Gulaid and he's there to stay.

I don't half feel relieved. Back in August war was breaking out between the family of one of my best mates and the firm my dad works for. So there was yours truly smack in the middle of No Man's Land dodging shells. Maybe Dad'll even resurface. I think he's in a nark with me for taking Bashir's side. He's weird that way. Clears off on us for all those years but still thinks we owe him. He does nothing for it but he still expects our blind loyalty. He could take a few lessons from Mum. She's always there and she never asks for anything in return. I feel rotten sometimes. Mum would move the world for us and it's still my dad I go on about. I can't help it, though. No matter how many times he hurts me, I can't help the way I feel. I still need him in my life. I'm just keeping my fingers crossed. If things stay quiet on the Parade, maybe Dad will get over it and come and see us. Well, I can hope, can't I?

Four

Chris left Kev, Jamie and Bashir at the Bollards that sliced South Road in half. The concrete barrier had been erected by the council to stop lorries using the estate as a short cut. And as a measure against the joyriders who took to the roads after dark. It didn't do much good. Deep tyre tracks in the muddy verges showed that the drivers simply mounted the pavements to get round the obstruction. But Chris wasn't bothered about traffic or joyriders. To him the bollards marked the border of Diamonds' territory. He remained an outsider for now, but in eight days all that would change.

'See you lads,' he called.

'See you, Chris,' they responded.

He was twenty yards away when Kev shouted after him. 'Hey, Cheryl says you move in a week tomorrow.'

'That's right.'

'We're looking forward to it,' said Kev. 'We'll have a good crack.'

'You bet.'

The shower that had been threatening all morning broke with a vengeance, heavy rain bursting from banks of violet clouds. Chris turned up his collar and hurried on. 'Can't make its mind up,' he told himself. 'First the sun's cracking the flags, then this.' As if to prove the point, the downpour abated and the sun emerged from the stormclouds, raking the drenched streets with garish light. Moments later a rainbow appeared. It was faint and faded into the darkness overhead but the stubby arch that defied the clouds was brilliant in the sunlight. Chris stopped and stared. Half a rainbow. The promise of something, then darkness.

The story of his life. He hoped it wouldn't be the same with the Diamonds. Another false dawn would be just too much.

'Half twelve,' he told himself, consulting his watch. 'Time I was back. Gerwyn won't be happy if I'm not back for Sunday dinner.'

Cook was still off so he was in for a Gerwyn special. Pork done so well it looked like it had come out of the barrel of a flame-thrower. Double roasties too. As he stepped up his pace he noticed two boys on the other side of the road. A couple of Costello's crew. What were their names? Yes, Carl and Mattie, that was it. Deliberately shortening his stride, he affected nonchalance, digging his hands deep into his pockets. It was the same drill whenever he came up against kids who might try it on. Look cocky enough to give them pause for thought, but not so much they felt forced to knock it out of you. Carl and Mattie were crossing the road.

'Here we go,' he said under his breath. He weighed his sports bag in his right hand. Heavy enough to make a handy weapon.

'Well, look who it isn't,' said Carl loudly.

Keep it cool. Don't do anything silly. It's two on to one.

'Chris Flower, isn't it?' said Mattie.

'Or is it Cower?' said Carl. 'It was you I saw curled up on the floor the other day, wasn't it?'

Chris stared straight ahead and carried on walking. *Look hard. Don't make eye contact. They're not that sure of themselves.* As he drew level with them, Chris squeezed the handles of the bag. Just in case.

'Not talking, Power?' asked Carl.

Don't rise to it. Just walk on nice and steady, but be ready to hit back. They'd stopped. A few more steps and they were staring at his back.

'What's up; cat got your tongue?'

That's it, keep on going. They're not going to do anything now. The moment's gone. He was in sight of the main road. Turn left, five minutes' walk and he would be home. *A quick glance back. Just to be sure.* Chris wasn't about to be caught napping. Imagine if they were meeting the rest of their gang. It was only at the flyover that he finally felt safe. Five minutes later he was sitting down to his Sunday dinner. Or lunch, as cook insisted on calling it. But cook wasn't there so new rules applied.

'I'm with you, Chris,' Gerwyn announced. 'It's definitely dinner.'

Chris smiled. Half a rainbow, eh? It was a start.

'Are you looking forward to it?' asked Crusty as they got ready for bed. 'The move, I mean.'

'Dunno.' Then, after a moment's thought: 'Yes, maybe I am.'

'They're all right then, these ...' Crusty searched his memory for the name. 'These Tasker people?'

'You never know until you have to live with them.'

Chris remembered another attempt at fostering. A house in West Derby. A short, stocky man in cords and a lumberjack shirt and his emulsion-white wife. It was a placement made in Hell. He'd hated them from the start. Them and their two stupid dachshunds. If you're going to have a dog, make it a proper one. One that eats postmen – whole. It wasn't that they actually did anything especially wrong. It was the way they were so rotten *caring* all the time. It was like they were on a time-switch. If he went ten seconds without smiling they would come up and ask what was wrong.

'Still,' said Chris, banishing thoughts of Mr and Mrs Dachsund. 'I bet the Taskers don't go in my stuff.'

'Oh, give me a break,' said Crusty. 'I've said sorry, haven't I? What do you want me to do, get down on my hands and knees?'

'Now that I'd like to see,' said Chris.

Crusty smiled. 'I got you something,' he said. 'Sort of to say sorry for nicking your gear all the time.' He held out a carrier bag.

'You didn't rob it, did you?' asked Chris suspiciously.

'Of course not,' said Crusty. 'The receipt's inside.'

'It's from the Everton club shop!' cried Chris, accepting the present. 'How did you afford this?'

Crusty shrugged his shoulders. 'I get pocket money.'

'Not much,' said Chris. He knew it must have taken him weeks to save this much.

'It's all right, isn't it?' asked Crusty. 'It is Everton you like? I'm not into footy myself.'

'Of course it's right,' said Chris, pulling out the blue scarf. 'Crusty, I could kiss you.'

'Steady on now,' said Crusty, blushing.

'I *was* joking,' said Chris.

'Sure, I know that.'

After a few moments he cleared his throat. 'Chris.'

'Yes?'

'It isn't just to say sorry.'

Another uncomfortable pause. 'I'm trying to tell you I'll miss you.'

'But I batter you!'

'I've had worse.'

Chris laughed. 'Crusty,' he said. 'You're an original.' As he wrapped the scarf round his neck he remembered the goal line clearance and the way he'd left the gang behind. Suddenly bits of rainbow were popping up all over the place.

Five

Kev arrived home whistling.

'Somebody's happy,' said Mum.

'What do you expect?' said Kev. 'We won. I scored the winning goal.'

'That's great.' Her smile was a brief one. It flickered like the morning's sunny intervals, then died. Kev's insides shifted. What now?

'Something up?'

'Your dad's here. He's in the living room with Gareth.'

Kev frowned. Better late than never. Just. 'What does he want?'

A noncommittal shrug from Mum. 'He's come to take you out.'

Kev felt a tremor of excitement. Even if it was mixed with more than a touch of resentment at another of Dad's disappearing acts. 'Take us out? Makes a change. I wonder what he's after.' Mum gave a little shake of the head, then looked over Kev's shoulder. Kev heard a man's tread on the hall floor behind him.

'What makes you think I'm after something?' Dad asked. 'Can't a man take his sons out for the day?'

'Of course you can,' said Kev. 'So what's been stopping you for the last couple of weeks? I thought you'd forgotten we existed.' He was secretly overjoyed to see Dad, but he wasn't about to let it show. The old man had let him down too often for that. Let him stew for a bit.

'I suppose I asked for that,' said Dad. 'I had business.'

'Sure,' said Kev. 'Business.'

In his mind's eye Kev could see Dad in the driver's

seat of Lee Ramage's BMW. On business. He had a good idea how Dad made his money. The stuff he was into made him a candidate for *Crimewatch* – and not as a copper, either!

'So where are we going?'

'Pictures?'

Dad waved the *Echo* cinema guide under his nose. 'Will this one be all right?'

'A bit young,' said Kev grudgingly. Actually, he'd been dying to see the film for weeks, but Dad was going to have to work to get back in his good books.

'Tough,' said Dad. 'It's got to be something Gareth will like too.'

Kev watched his kid brother struggling with his laces. 'Here,' he said. 'Let me.'

'The lad should be able to tie his laces by now,' said Dad. 'Nearly six, aren't you Gareth?'

Mum bridled. 'Don't lecture me on bringing up the boys, Tony,' she snapped. 'You've no right. You were never around.'

Kev and Gareth exchanged dismayed glances. Not a fight. Not now. Dad ignored Mum's words. It was typical of him. He didn't bat an eyelid. The truth was something he could parry as well as any punch.

'So what about the film, Kev?' he asked.

'It'll do, I suppose. So long as you take us for something to eat afterwards.'

'McDonalds?' asked Gareth.

'Nah,' said Kev. 'Not enough choice, and the puddings are boring. What about an American diner? The chips are just like McDonalds,' he told Gareth. 'And I can have an all-day breakfast.' He could almost taste the pancakes and maple syrup. He hadn't eaten out since Jamie's dad had taken them after fishing one Sunday afternoon.

'OK,' said Gareth. 'Do they have ice-cream?'

'Yes, great big ones in a glass. They come with all the trimmings.'

'What, like little flags?'

'That's right. Stars and stripes.'

Gareth smiled. He was converted.

'That's the deal then,' said Kev. 'Film and a meal.'

'Done,' said Dad. 'See you later, Carol.'

Mum smiled thinly. Kev could read her face. Typical of Dad. Leave her to bring up the boys alone then descend on them to spend more in a day than she had to live on in a week. Kev was dying to say something, aching to let her know how he felt, but the words just wouldn't come. Instead, he just followed Dad out of the door.

'No car?' asked Kev as they walked towards South Parade.

'Lee's got it,' said Dad. 'I'll pick up a cab.' At the mention of Lee Ramage's name, Kev looked away. He didn't appreciate being reminded of Dad's low-life boss.

'What's up with your face all of a sudden?' Dad demanded.

'Nothing.'

'Not much, there isn't,' said Dad in a tone of voice that had Gareth looking nervous. 'The business I do with Lee is paying for your day out, lad. And don't you forget it.'

Kev would have loved to forget it. Just like he wanted to forget the way Dad had cleared off on the family for four long years.

'I'm hardly likely to,' said Kev.

When they arrived at South Parade Dad waved to a man leaning against a private-hire taxi. Kev glanced at the plate. *Ramage taxis*. Another of Lee Ramage's hooky sidelines. 'Where to, Tony?'

'The MGM multiplex. Call back for us about four.'

The driver's face fell. 'What if I have a fare?'

'Give it to somebody else,' said Dad, stamping his authority. 'Or have you forgotten it's me and Lee who pay your wages?'

'I haven't forgotten,' said the driver dully. Kev stole a glance at Dad. The performance was for his and Gareth's benefit, of course. He was showing off. The Big Man. Up to his ears in money and *business*. The trouble was, much as Kev tried not to let it show, he was loving every minute of it.

'Another dessert?' asked Dad.

'I'll have a lollipop,' said Gareth. 'They keep them in jars behind the counter.'

'What about you, Kev?'

'No, I'm stuffed.' Stuffed was right. It was the second plate of fudge brownies that did it. Or maybe the double choc ice-cream that went with it.

'Here,' said Dad, digging into the back pocket of his jeans. 'Do you want to do me a favour, Gareth?'

'What?'

'Go and pay the bill, son.' Dad produced a roll of tenners and peeled off three. 'You can ask them for your lollipop while you're there.'

Gareth looked at the queue. He clearly didn't fancy the idea of going on his own. 'Can't you come with me?'

'Oh, you're a big boy now,' said Dad.

'I'm only five.'

Kev smiled. When Gareth wanted to play out he was *nearly six*. When he was asked to do something like this he was *only five*.

'Go on, son. You'll be OK.'

'I'll take him,' Kev offered.

'No,' said Dad. 'Let Gareth do it. Here's our bill. You'll have to give it to the woman along with the money.' Gareth nodded and nervously slid out of their booth.

'Was that to get rid of him?' asked Kev.

'Not soft, are you lad?'

'So what is it you don't want him to hear?'

Dad hesitated for a few moments. 'It's about that mate of yours. The ... black kid.'

'Bashir? What about him?'

'It's the way you stuck up for him when I had that do with his old feller? That hurt, Kev. A man expects loyalty from his own son.'

Kev's heart jerked. He'd been waiting for something like this. 'It wasn't fair,' Kev replied. 'What's Mr Gulaid ever done to you, Dad? I don't get it.'

'He's an inconvenience,' said Dad. 'You'd be better steering clear.'

Kev balled a fist. 'I won't, and you can't make me. Bashir's my mate.' Then pointedly: 'He sticks by me.'

Dad shook his head. 'Not good at choosing your friends, are you lad?'

'That's rich coming from you!' cried Kev, attracting the attention of some of the other customers.

'Keep it down,' said Dad. 'You're making a show of us.'

'No Dad,' said Kev defiantly. 'You're making a show of us. You always have.'

'It's about time you got yourself sorted, son. You don't go against your own blood. It was wrong, putting that kid ahead of me.'

Kev was almost shaking. With anger, but also with

fear. What if he said too much? What if Dad walked away – for good, this time?

'Yeah?' he said, his voice shaking. 'Well, I was only doing what I thought was right.'

'You're making a mistake, Kev,' said Dad. 'You'll get nowhere sticking up for losers.'

'Oh, and you're a winner, I suppose?'

Dad patted the pocket where he kept his roll of ten-pound notes. 'That's right.'

'Is that all you care about, Dad – money?'

'Makes the world go round, Kev. You're no good without it.'

'That's the difference between you and me,' Kev answered. He thought of Chris. Maybe this wasn't that much better than having no dad at all. 'You'll do anything for money. Me, I think there's other things that matter. Your mates … your family. You let people down. I don't.'

Dad reacted sharply, like the words had jolted him back in his seat. He stared at Kev, eyes hard with anger. 'If that's the way you feel, there's nothing more to say. I'll drop you off home.'

'You do that Dad,' said Kev. He was shaking and feeling sick inside. 'But don't expect me to change. Bash is my mate.'

Dad continued to stare at him. 'You do know Lee won't stand for Gulaid's nonsense, don't you? Sooner or later, he's going to sort him.'

Kev's heart kicked. 'Has he said something?'

'Not yet, but he isn't happy. Mark my words, Lee won't back off. There's nothing down for your Mr Gulaid.'

'And you'll help Ramage do it?'

'It's my job.'

Kev was fighting back the tears. 'You can't do this, Dad. It's not fair. He's running a shop, that's all.'

'In the wrong place at the wrong time,' said Dad. 'Lee tried to buy him out. He made a generous offer. Old Gooly wouldn't listen.'

It was Kev's turn to be angry. 'Don't talk about him like that!'

'There you go again,' said Dad. 'Putting his sort before your own father.'

Kev was about to protest, but Gareth was back. 'What's wrong?' he asked.

'Nothing,' said Kev. 'Nothing at all.'

Dad took the change from Gareth. 'Let's go,' he said.

As they walked to the car Gareth slipped his hand into Kev's for reassurance. 'What's wrong?' he asked again.

'Nothing,' said Kev. But the real answer was – everything.

Six

Suddenly I know how the Japanese feel.

I saw this old film on cable round Jamie's. Seven Samurai or something. Seems they had paper houses in Japan in those days. I could imagine it. You build yourself this brilliant house and you think you've got a real home. Four walls, a family. You're safe. Then along come the bad guys and start wrecking it. That's when you realize. It isn't safe at all, just paper.

That's the story of my life. Maybe there's Japanese blood in me somewhere. The only trouble is, one of the bad guys beating down the walls is my own dad. Doesn't he realize what he's doing? Doesn't he even care? Just when I thought I had something going for me, just when I was starting to feel good about myself, along he comes and socks a hole through my world. The question is, what do I do about it? Should I warn Bash and risk losing Dad, or keep quiet and maybe put my best mate's family in danger?

I wish the whole thing would go away. What did I do to deserve all this? It's like I was cursed at birth.

Seven

Chris looked suspiciously at the cardboard tube.

'What's this?'

'What do you think it is?' said Kev, continuing to hold it out. 'A present.'

'What for?'

'Call it a house-warming gift.'

Chris looked around his new room. A single divan, an MFI wardrobe, a computer desk (minus computer), a bedside table and a lamp with a small tear in the shade. No great shakes, but it was his. Or so the Taskers kept telling him. 'You sure?'

'Of course I'm sure,' said Kev. 'I wouldn't be giving it to you if I wasn't.'

Chris took the tube and peeled the strip of sellotape sealing the end. 'It's a poster.'

'That's right,' said Kev. 'Well, aren't you going to have a look?'

Chris slid it out and unrolled it. 'It's the first team squad! Excellent.'

'Pity they're not doing better on the field,' said Kev. 'But we're true Blues. We'll follow them through thick and thin.'

'Guv, this is great.'

Kev smiled. 'I thought you needed something to brighten up the room. Something to make it your own.' He handed Chris a blob of Blu-tak and watched him hanging the poster.

'It's not till you get your own stuff that people get the message,' Kev continued. 'This is my turf. Steer clear.'

Chris thought of Crusty and nodded his head. His own turf. Could it really be true?

'Are you up there?' called Cheryl.

'Yes,' Kev answered. 'In Chris's room. Why, what are you after?'

'Mum and Dad want you downstairs.'

Kev glanced at Chris. 'Sounds ominous,' he said. 'I wonder what we've done wrong?'

Chris tensed.

'Hey, I was only joking,' said Kev. 'Lighten up, will you?'

Chris nodded, but he wasn't really the lightening-up type. Still apprehensive over the joke, he followed Kev into the kitchen.

'What's this?' he asked, his eyes fastening on a cake with a single candle.

Kev laughed. 'That's all you ever say,' he told Chris.

'But what is it? What's it for?'

Uncle Dave pointed theatrically to the candle. 'Day one in your new home,' he said.

Chris stared. Kev recognized the expression. He'd gone all moody this way before he blew in the school playground.

'You shouldn't be doing this,' said Chris, frowning. 'It isn't right.'

It was uncle Dave's turn to frown. 'Why on earth not?'

— 73 —

'You shouldn't build things up,' Chris replied. 'They just end up going wrong.'

Uncle Dave and aunty Pat exchanged glances. Cheryl hung around in the background wearing her this'll-end-in-tears look.

'At least blow the candle out,' said aunty Pat hopefully.

'Yes, OK,' said Chris. 'If it makes you happy.' He watched the extinguished candle smoking.

'Sorry if that was a bit naff,' said uncle Dave. 'We just wanted you to know how delighted we are to have you here.' Cheryl slurped noisily from her milk shake. Just to let everyone know the sentiment wasn't unanimous.

'Thanks,' said Chris, his eyes still fastened on the cake. 'It's just …'

Cheryl shook her head and walked out of the kitchen. Unfazed, Chris mumbled out the rest of the sentence.

'… I didn't expect anything.'

The truth was, he never did.

'I'd better be off in a minute,' said Kev, looking out at the streetlights flickering across the Diamond. 'Mum's got a bee in her bonnet over this homework business. Thinks if I do it all on time I'll end up as an airline pilot or a company executive. Dole-ite's more like it.'

'Jailbird, you mean,' said Chris, absent-mindedly.

'Come again?'

Chris bit his lip. 'Forget it.'

Kev gave him a puzzled look.

'Forget it.' Chris repeated.

'OK, OK,' said Kev, holding up his hands. 'It's forgotten.'

There was an uneasy silence, then Chris spoke again. 'I'll tell you if you like.'

Kev continued to look out at the evening sky. 'No need.'

'No, I want to.'

'Don't do me any favours.'

Chris tossed his pillow at Kev's back. The Guv'nor could be as touchy as he was. 'Hey, do you want to know or not?' Kev was still acting prickly.

'If you like.'

Chris took a deep breath. 'It's my dad. He's inside.'

Kev snapped to attention. 'What for?'

'He was going after some feller. You know, a grudge.'

'He was going to batter him?'

'Break his legs, more like. He had a baseball bat.'

'What was it over?'

Chris sighed. 'Robbing, dealing. The coppers raided our flat and found loads of knocked-off gear. You know the score.'

'Yes,' said Kev. 'I know all right.' He saw Chris looking at him inquiringly.

'My old feller's the same.'

'What, he's in nick?'

Kev shook his head. 'No, but he could be heading that way.' It was his turn to be uncomfortable. 'So where's your mum?'

This time, Chris shut up shop completely. Questions about Dad he could handle. Mum was forbidden territory. 'None of your business.' His eyes were hooded, brooding.

'Sorry. I was only wondering.'

'Well, don't.' Chris's voice was hard.

'Whoa,' said Kev. 'Keep your hair on. I'm out of here.' He picked up his coat and swung it over his shoulder. He'd reached the doorway before Chris recovered from his rush of blood.

'Guv.'

'Yes?'

'I'm not being funny. It's just ...'

'Forget it,' said Kev. 'It doesn't bother me. I shouldn't have stuck my nose in. Mr Nosy, that's me.'

'Just what I was thinking.'

'Chris,' said Kev, trying not to react. 'I understand. See you in the morning.'

'Yes,' said Chris. 'See you at school.'

Kev was halfway down the stairs when he started to go over the little scene in his mind. He understood all right. They really were brothers under the skin.

Eight

It was Friday before things started to go pear-shaped. 7S were lined up outside Room 18 waiting for Mrs Spinks and Personal and Social Education when the gang walked past.

'Got a new sidekick, have you McGovern?' asked Costello without giving Chris a second glance.

'Staying at your Cheryl's, I hear,' said Brain Damage. 'How come? Got no family of his own?' They were probing for weakness, and Kev knew it. Kev rested a hand on Chris's arm. Unobtrusively, so the gang didn't see the attempt at restraint.

'What happened?' asked Brain Damage. 'Mislay them somewhere?'

'Not to worry,' said Costello. 'I hear the Sally Army run a Lost and Found – Parents R Us. You never know Power, you could always pick one up cheap.'

Kev sensed Chris's anger. The slow burn had begun.

'I tell you what, though,' said Brain Damage,

delivering his line in an obviously well-rehearsed routine. 'Losing one parent is careless …'

'But losing two,' said Costello. 'That's criminal.' They planted themselves in front of Chris, waiting for a reaction. They got it, but not from Chris.

'Take a hike,' said Kev.

'Yes,' said Jamie. 'Get lost.' The poison pair had back up. Carl, Mattie, Tez and Jelly Wobble hovered, looking ugly. It didn't take any effort.

'I thought I told you to move,' said Kev, taking a step forward.

But Costello was ready for him. 'Keep your shirt on,' he quipped.

At the mention of his beloved Everton shirt, Kev's face went white with anger. 'Think you're funny, do you Costello? Well, how's about I give you something to laugh about.' He balled his fists.

'Sorry,' said Costello, not even blinking an eyelid. 'I'd like to oblige, but not this morning.' With that the gang sauntered away, pleased with the impact they'd made.

'Oh, by the way,' said Brain Damage, pausing at the end of the corridor. 'I hear your old feller and our Lee used to be sparring partners, Power.'

Kev stared at Chris. This was news to him.

'So how is prison food these days?' Chris didn't say a word. His face said it all.

'What was that about?' asked Ratso as the gang turned the corner.

'Ignore them,' said Kev hurriedly. He hadn't told anybody what he knew about Chris. 'It's just a wind-up.'

'Funny thing to say, though,' said Jamie.

'Sure,' grunted Chris. 'Flipping hysterical.'

'You OK?' asked Kev. Curiosity was eating away at

him. Just what was the link between Chris's dad and Lee Ramage? It would have to go on the back-burner, however. Mrs Spinks had arrived.

'Right,' she said, unlocking the classroom door. 'In you go.'

Throughout registration Chris sat with his head bowed.

'Do you think he's all right?' whispered Jamie.

'Of course,' Kev replied. But he wasn't so sure.

Mrs Spinks got to Chris's name on the register. 'Chris Power.' No answer.

'Chris?' Ratso leaned across and tapped Chris on the arm.

'What?'

Ratso indicated Mrs Spinks.

'I've just called your name,' she told him. But the brush with the gang had taken Chris over the edge. Kev recognized the look in his eyes. 'You are here then?' ventured Mrs Spinks, making light of his behaviour.

'Stupid question.'

Mrs Spinks hesitated, wondering how to react. 'I'll mark you present,' she said, deciding to avoid a confrontation.

'Cool it eh, Chris,' said Kev. 'She's only calling the register.' But Chris didn't want to know him either. He just looked away.

Jamie nudged Kev. 'Doesn't take much to set him off, does it?' Kev shrugged his shoulders. He was starting to feel anxious.

'Now,' said Mrs Spinks, closing the register. 'I'd like you to spend five minutes silently reading this passage. Peter ...' She was looking at Ratso. 'Would you hand these out please?' Ratso nodded and darted around placing a pamphlet on everyone's desk.

'What's this?' said Jamie.

'One of those council things,' said Kev. 'Smoking, drugs. Just Say No.'

'I said,' Mrs Spinks reminded them, '*Silent* reading.' Kev glanced at Chris. He hadn't even opened his booklet. It was obvious from Mrs Spinks' expression that this irritated her. But she let it ride. For now. 'You should have got the gist by now,' she said after a few minutes. 'Opinions anybody?'

Jacqui Bell put her hand up. 'It's saying that smoking and drugs are bad for you,' she said. Snorts of derision from the back.

'Somebody laughed at that,' said Mrs Spinks. 'Why? Anybody like to tell us?' She scanned the class. 'Anybody?' But there were no takers.

'Jamie,' she said. 'You've usually got something to say.'

Jamie pulled a face. Put your hand up once and you're a marked man. 'Like Jacqui said, they're bad for you.'

'So,' Mrs Spinks asked, 'Why do so many people do it? Smoke, take drugs?'

A few hands went up. To show you're big. To act cool. Because it's fun.

'Why's it fun?'

'You get a buzz,' said Kev.

'But drugs can kill you,' said Jacqui.

'So can cars,' said Kev. 'Nobody bans them.'

'But that's different,' Jacqui protested. As the discussion continued Kev was aware of Chris shifting in his seat.

Jacqui's friend Melanie had just joined the fray. 'It's the dealers who are the problem,' she said.

That's when Chris spoke up for the first time. 'You don't know what you're talking about.'

'Yes I do,' Melanie insisted. 'You see them on our estate.'

'It's a business,' said Chris. 'Like any other.'

'But is it like any other?' asked Mrs Spinks. 'It's against the law for a start.' Chris laughed. It was an angry, sneering laugh. 'What's so funny?'

'You are.' Mrs Spinks just looked at him. Like Kev she had started to sense that the discussion could get out of hand. 'So's this,' said Chris, waving the booklet. 'Do-gooder rubbish.'

'Oh, come on Chris,' she said. 'You've got to do better than that.' She approached him. 'Pick something you disagree with.' Chris lowered his eyes. He didn't like her close to him.

Leave it, Spinksy, Kev pleaded silently.

But Mrs Spinks was determined to plough on. 'One sentence. Anything.' She reached for Chris's booklet. He jerked it away.

'Get off!' He started tearing up the hated booklet. 'I only ...'

Chris didn't want to listen. Tossing the remains of the booklet on the floor he interrupted her: 'Get out of my face.'

'Chris,' she said, trying to calm him, 'Let's just ...'

He stood up abruptly. 'You deaf?' he shouted. 'Leave me alone.'

'Sit down, please,' she said, desperate to assert herself. 'Or I'll have to give you a disruption slip.'

Chris's face twisted. 'Oh, do what you like.'

Mrs Spinks headed for her stockroom where she kept her slips. She unlocked the door and stepped inside. Chris was up immediately, following her. As she disappeared for a moment into the room, he closed the door and turned the key that was sticking invitingly out of the lock. Mrs Spinks started knocking, demanding to be released. Chris took no notice. Without a moment's hesitation, he walked to the window and flung the key outside.

Kev watched in amazement for a few seconds before stating the obvious: 'That's torn it.'

Nine

I thought uncle Dave would go ballistic, but I was wrong. He just picked Chris up from the office and took him home. The funny thing is, Scarisbrick's got dead strict rules, but the Head of Year didn't do anything. Not even a suspension. It's like the school is bending over backwards with Chris. But why? I don't get it. I was so curious, I called in straight after school last night to see how Chris was, but he was up in his room. He didn't want to see anybody. Cheryl was the one who was really wound up over it. She reckons she'll never be able to show her face in school again. Talk about over-reacting! It is worrying though, the way Chris can take off like that. I mean, this stuff between him and Brain Damage, it's really heavy. And Dad's mixed up in it somewhere. This is really starting to crack me up. It's like I'm walking into a minefield – blindfolded! I know Ronnie was impressed by the way Chris defended against St Bede's, but I'm worried. Ronnie seems to have him pencilled in for a start tomorrow. We're playing Sefton Dynamoes and Joey Bannen's cried off with a dose of the flu. I should be happy for Chris but there's something not quite right. If Chris flips it could really sour things for us. I just don't think we can take the risk in an important match. I'll have to let Ronnie know what he's like. I know, I know, it sounds like I'm ratting on a mate, but I've got to think about the team. A win against

Sefton and a good result the week after against last year's runners-up Ajax Aintree and we could be contesting the top spot. Nobody, but nobody is going to get in the way of that. Not even my brother under the skin.

Ten

Kev didn't like the atmosphere in the dressing room that Sunday morning. Chris's little lock-up trick meant instant street cred. He was quite the hero.

'He did what?' chortled Conor as he folded his Adidas top.

'Locked the old biddy in her own stock cupboard,' said Ratso. 'You should have seen her when Jacqui Bell got the key and let her out. Bright red she was.'

'Nothing like that happens in our school, does it Liam?'

The Savage twins lived in the terraces on the other side of the flyover from the Diamond, so they weren't at Scarisbrick. They went to Brightside instead. 'No, the most excitement we've had was when that dog got into school.'

'Did you get suspended?' asked Conor, showing Chris new respect.

But Chris was doing nothing to feed the excitement. 'No,' he grunted.

'What, not even one day?'

'No.'

'They must be dead soft at Scarisbrick,' Conor observed. 'You don't get away with anything at Brightside.'

'They're usually like that at ours,' said Jamie. 'Funny, isn't it Guv?'

'Sure,' said Kev sarcastically. 'Look at me laughing.' He didn't like the way the conversation was going. 'Now, if you've quite finished we've got a match to win. Or have you forgotten we're only three points off the top?'

'Joking, aren't you Guv?' said Ratso. Then, donning his Statto hat: 'There's only three teams above us. Northend have a point over us. Longmoor and Ajax are joint top. The only teams with a 100 per cent record.'

The table flashed up in Kev's mind:

	Played	*Won*	*Drawn*	*Lost*	*Points*
	Pl	**W**	**D**	**L**	**Pts**
Ajax Aintree	4	4	0	0	12
Longmoor Celtic	4	4	0	0	12
Northend United	4	3	1	0	10
Rough Diamonds	4	3	0	1	9

'So it's vital we win, lads,' said Kev.

'My sentiments exactly,' came a voice. Ronnie had just walked in. 'They got the double over us last year remember. They've got a good midfield and they like to pack the centre of the park, so what have we got to do, lads?'

'Get wide,' was the unanimous reply.

'Clever boys,' said Ronnie with a grin.

'You do say it every week, uncle Ron,' Jimmy reminded him.

'Correct,' said Ronnie, 'But you don't do it every week. It's something we still fall down on. We try to build through the middle, running into the opposition where they're strongest. We've got to get behind this outfit, and we've got the lads to do it. Bashir, I want you to really attack them. Liam, I'm playing you as a wingback. I want you to get forward as much as you can and give Bash the support he needs.' Liam nodded eagerly. It was his first start and the brief was right down his alley. 'Jimmy, you'll be doing the same on the right. Jamie, I want you to go wide if you have to. Leave Conor to act as the target man.'

Jamie wrinkled his nose. And give the big-headed nerd all the best chances, he thought. 'Why Conor?'

'Because he's bigger, stronger and a better header of the ball,' Ronnie replied. 'Your strength is your footwork, Jamie. Play to it.' Conor's smile was so wide you could have driven a tank through it. 'OK, lads,' said Ronnie. 'Let's do it.' Kev was about to follow the others out of the changing room when Ronnie called him back. 'Kev, I thought I should let you know. There's a scout here today. He's looking you and Daz over.'

Kev's heart lurched. 'A scout. Who from? The Blues?'

'Sorry lad, no such luck. He's from Crewe Alex, but they've got a good set-up down there. Do your best.' Kev nodded. The Diamonds took the field to the tune of *Three Lions*. Ratso's ghetto-blaster anthems were a familiar feature at Jacob's Lane.

'Let's hope the opposition slip up,' said Ant as the teams took up position. He glanced at the other five games going on simultaneously.

'Forget what they're doing,' said Kev. He checked on Chris. He didn't look too upset to be sitting on the sidelines. It might be different if he knew Kev had weighed in against him getting a game. Relieved that Chris was taking his second stint on the bench so well, he turned back to Ant. 'No sense bothering about anybody else,' he said. 'We just need to play our own game.'

And that's exactly what the Diamonds did. Right from the off they unsettled the Dynamoes with biting tackles and some neat inter-passing. Most of the team were comfortable on the ball and hungry for possession. What's more, Conor was dominant in the air, winning almost every header.

'Some player eh, Jamie?' said Jimmy after Conor had hit the side netting with a fierce drive.

'Yes,' Jamie replied grudgingly. 'Some player.'

Midway through the half Bashir's pace was unsettling the Dynamoes defenders. Twice he was able to get to the goal line and deliver tempting crosses into the box. The first was headed wide by Conor. The second found the target, but Kev had been stretching and his shot lacked the power to beat the keeper.

'We should be ahead by now,' grumbled Jamie. 'It's Conor. He's too selfish by half.'

'We'll crack them,' said Kev. 'They don't know how to handle Bashir at all. As for Conor, I think he's having a pretty good game.'

Jamie just scowled. 'I still think he's selfish.'

'You've got a right to your opinion,' said Kev, before adding with typical cockiness. 'It's wrong, that's all.' That's when he noticed Chris pacing the touch line. He had that dark, brooding look again. Maybe he wasn't as happy as he'd seemed. Kev frowned. Even he found Chris's moods hard to take.

There wasn't time to dwell on Chris though. Liam was driving down the left: 'Now,' Kev said out loud, 'This looks promising.' Liam cut infield, taking two defenders with him then laid the ball off with the outside of his boot. Running on to the pass Bashir hit it first time into the box. Just when it looked to be reaching Jamie unmarked on the far post, Conor stuck out a boot. The ball skidded inches wide.

'You divvy!' he yelled, venting his anger. 'If you'd stepped over it I'd have been left with a simple tap-in.' Conor grinned and jogged away.

'See that,' said Jamie, 'He couldn't care less.'

Kev slapped Jamie on the back. 'Nearly scored though, didn't he?' It was as he returned to the halfway line that Kev remembered the scout. He spotted him talking to Ronnie. They were looking in Kev's direction. It was the spur he needed to throw himself into the midfield scramble with even more enthusiasm. Coming away with the ball, he looked up and saw Conor leading his marker a merry chase. 'Con,' he shouted, flighting a pass downfield.

Conor took the ball on his chest, turned his man and ran across the edge of the penalty area, attracting another Dynamoes defender. At the same time the keeper was advancing off the line. It was now or never. Curling his foot round the ball Conor hit it low under the goalie's body. One–nil.

Of the forward players only Jamie held back from the celebrations. Two minutes later the Diamonds almost went two-up. The danger came from the right wing. It was Jimmy's turn to turn provider firing a low, skidding cross into the area. This time it was Conor who was clear and Jamie who went for goal when leaving it was the best option.

'Pathetic,' snapped Conor. 'Getting your own back, are you?'

Jamie shrugged his shoulders. 'What do you think?' As they continued sniping at each other, the Dynamoes hit the Diamonds on the break. With Jimmy stranded in the opposition's last third, Gord found himself exposed. Two attackers were bearing down on him. A neat one-two and they were past him and into the area.

Making up ground quickly, Kev knew his tackle had to be a good one. Catch the man and it was a penalty.

'Yes!' Perfect contact on the ball. Unfortunately, the ref thought otherwise. The Dynamoes' striker Steve Wilson crashed theatrically to the ground. The ref hesitated for a moment then pointed to the spot.

'No way,' Kev shouted. 'I got the ball. He dived.' The ref waved away his protests. Daz could do nothing about the spot-kick. One–one, and that's how it was at halftime.

'Flipping great,' Kev fumed as he reached Ronnie. 'A scout comes and I concede a penalty.'

'I wouldn't worry,' said Ronnie. 'He was impressed.'

'So where is he now?'

'Taking a look at one of the Longmoor strikers.'

'Bobby Sutton?'

'Yes, that's the one.'

Kev went over to Chris. 'Picked up any halftime scores?' he asked.

'Ronnie did. Longmoor are winning two–nil. Ajax are being held one–one like us.'

'What about the Liver Bird?' asked Kev.

Chris grimaced. 'Winning two–one. Costello and Brain Damage were trying to wind me up just before you arrived.'

'Did they get anywhere?'

Chris gave Kev a sidelong glance. 'No.'

'Let's keep it like that.'

'I didn't plan to lock that teacher in the cupboard,' said Chris. 'I just get this rush of blood. I don't do it on purpose.'

'Maybe not,' said Kev. 'Still happened though, didn't it?' Chris lowered his eyes. As far as he was concerned it was conversation over. 'Looks like we're

about to restart,' said Kev. 'See you after the match.'
Chris didn't answer. OK, thought Kev, so sulk.

'What's up with Chris?' asked Ratso.

'Who knows?' Kev replied. 'But I'm glad Liam got
the nod over him. Chris wouldn't have been much use
to us in this mood.' He was glad he'd had that word
with Ronnie.

Eleven

The second half opened with the Diamonds stepping
up a gear. Conor in particular was proving a handful
for the Dynamoes defence. His downward headers and
flick-ons didn't give his markers the chance to get into
their stride.

'Good, isn't he?' said Ratso admiringly. Jamie kept
quiet.

'Why don't you push up, Guv?' asked Ant. 'We
don't need you covering us. They don't attack enough
for that.'

Kev nodded. 'I've just come to the same conclusion.'
As he jogged midway into the opposition half Kev
spotted an opening. One of the Dynamoes defenders
had pushed the ball too far as he brought it forward.
Kev nipped in smartly and dispossessed him.

'Guv!' yelled Conor making a forceful run towards
the penalty area. Sensing the danger to his goal his
marker scythed him down. Another yard and it would
have been a penalty.

'Who's taking the free kick?' asked Conor. He
obviously thought there could only be one answer. But
he was to be disappointed. Kev stood over the ball and
eyed the Dynamoes wall. The keeper was edging

toward the left, even though his defenders had that side well covered. Taking a couple of steps back, Kev advanced and curled the ball over the wall and into the top right-hand corner of the net. Two–one.

The immaculate set-piece had his team mates swarming all over him.

'Great goal, Guv,' enthused Ratso. Kev smiled, but there was a cloud over his enjoyment. That scout was still over at the Longmoor game watching Bobby Sutton. Just his luck! The Dynamoes made a couple of substitutions, bringing on more attack-minded players. It did little to change the balance of forces. The pace of Liam, Bashir and Jimmy was still opening up their defence at will and they weren't able to clear the ball long enough to put the Diamonds under pressure. A third goal was just a matter of time.

'Your ball,' said Kev rolling it into Liam's path. Liam looked up and spotted Conor making his run. His cross was at the perfect height for his twin brother. Rising to meet it, Conor glanced it towards the far post. The header had goal written all over it, but it wasn't to be credited to Conor. At the last moment Jamie scurried in to crash the ball into the roof of the net from close range. Three–one.

Jamie peeled away and threw himself full length on the turf in celebration. He was joined seconds later by Kev and Bashir.

'That should do it,' said Kev. 'I can't see them pulling two-back.'

As Jamie headed back to the centre circle Conor approached him. 'Hey you,' he said accusingly. 'That was my goal. It was already going in when you poached it.'

'I had to make certain,' Jamie replied. 'Predator's instinct.'

Conor glared at him. 'Predator my foot.'

The Diamonds were happy to play possession football for the last ten minutes.

'That was a good performance,' said Ronnie, greeting the team at the final whistle.

'Not bad,' said Kev. 'Pity about that chronic penalty decision. I like to keep a clean sheet.'

'Always the perfectionist, eh Guv,' said Ratso.

'No prizes for second best,' Kev answered. That's when he noticed that somebody was absent. 'Where's Chris?'

Dougie looked around. 'Funny, he was here a minute ago. Oh oh.'

'What?'

'Over there.' Chris was over on Pitch Five, eyeballing the Liver Birds team as they left the field.

'Ant, Jamie,' said Kev, 'Tag along with me just in case.'

'What are you up to?' Kev asked Chris.

'They started it,' Chris replied. 'They kicked off at me. For nothing.'

Costello laughed. 'We were only asking how your old feller was enjoying the food inside,' he said.

'And wondering if he remembers our Lee,' Brain Damage added. 'Lee remembers him.' Kev noticed that Brain Damage was in his track suit. He must have started his two-match suspension.

'Ignore them,' said Kev. 'They're not worth it.'

'Guv's right,' said Jamie. 'Come away.' As he and Ant guided Chris away, Costello said something that made the hairs on Kev's neck stand up.

'Hey Power, has McGovern told you about his old feller yet? That's right, Lee wasn't the only one who helped your dad book his ticket to the Costa Del Nick.'

Chris was some distance away and he didn't show

any signs of reacting. But Kev's face drained of blood. Surely Chris must have heard.

Twelve

I've been worrying about it all evening. Did Chris catch what Costello said? I mean, he didn't react or anything. No, I'm kidding myself. He must have done. Costello's a right foghorn. Mind you, if Chris did hear he's keeping pretty quiet about it. In fact, he hardly said a dicky bird all the way back to uncle Dave's. Not that that reassured me much. He doesn't always blow right away. The way I see it, he sometimes lets whatever's griping away inside him lie and fester. It just seems to eat into him until he can't take it any longer. Then he kicks off. That's how old Spinsky came to get it in the neck. Just my rotten luck, the moment the team starts to close on the front runners my stupid lousy dad comes back to haunt me. And it can only get worse. The gang are hardly likely to let it drop, are they? Sooner or later they're going to take another pop at Chris, and this time who knows what he'll do. There's no getting away from it, I'm going to have to face him with it. And soon. After all, if Dad is one of the reasons his old feller's banged away he's not going to like it. It's not that I'm scared. Sick is more like it. It makes my flesh creep, the idea of letting a mate down. Then there's the timing. The last thing we need is Chris going ape over something like this. It could really unsettle the team just before the big game with Ajax. I want to see Dad first, get it straight in my own mind. Though goodness knows how after our bust-up in the diner. Typical of Dad. Even when he isn't trying he manages to wreck everything. First it was Bash, now it's Chris. I always knew the old man was a liability. Now I'm starting to think he's one I just can't afford. But what on earth do I do? If I'm going to stop this damaging the Diamonds I need time. Just a little bit of time.

PART THREE

Catching Fire

One

By half-past five on Monday night Kev had started to feel that time might just be on his side. Chris hadn't mentioned Costello's little bombshell once.

'Are you with us, Kev?' shouted Ronnie.

'Me?' asked Kev. 'Sure, just thinking about next Sunday, that's all.' It wasn't the Ajax match that was on his mind. He was reliving the brief conversation with Dad. He'd caught up with him at Nan's. That's Nan McGovern, of course. His other gran wouldn't let Dad through the door. Blamed him for ruining Mum's life. Dad had been involved in the fit-up all right, the same way cows are involved with milk. He didn't show any remorse, of course. He was tight lipped about everything, what they were going to do about Bashir's dad, what had really happened to Chris's dad. All he would say, with a knowing grin, was that it had been easy to frame him. A doddle. *Power? Flower, more like.* He was short with Kev, and brutal about Chris's dad. *A loser,* he called him. That was just before Dad went off with Lee Ramage. Takes one to know one, thought Kev bitterly.

'We'll talk about Sunday in a few minutes,' said Ronnie. 'Now concentrate on defending this cross.' Ronnie really had a thing about crosses just lately. He was convinced that his wingers and wingbacks were the key to beating the top teams. 'OK Liam,' he called. 'Let's see what you can do.'

Kev glanced in the direction of Joey Bannen. He had recovered from the flu, but there was no guarantee he'd make the starting line-up. Liam had definitely impressed in the Dynamoes game.

'I want you to deliver the ball into the target area as Jamie and Conor make their runs,' Ronnie instructed. 'Don't loft it too high. Plenty of space. Just remember, any deflection can put the goal under threat.'

'He's been at the coaching manual again,' hissed Ratso.

The penalty area was crowded with defenders, just as Ronnie had ordered, but that didn't stop Liam. Striking the ball with his instep he bent the ball round the back of the defence. Kev managed to put enough pressure on Conor to prevent the goal, but in a competitive match it would have gone down as a chance.

'Good,' said Ronnie. 'Now it's your turn Joey.' By the look on his face Joey didn't fancy his chances. Gathering the ball from Ant, he ran forward and lashed at it. To his dismay it rocketed out of play.

'Gather round, lads,' said Ronnie.

'Who's getting the nod?' asked Daz anxiously. Joey was his best mate and he had a good idea how Ronnie's mind worked. It didn't look good.

'Eleven of our best,' Ronnie answered drily.

'No,' Daz insisted. 'Really. Right back's the only position that's open to doubt.'

'That right?' said Ronnie. 'Then you know more than me.' He was a stickler for routine and nobody was going to get him to change. 'Daz in goal,' he began.

'Surprise surprise,' said Ant.

'The back four,' Ronnie continued, 'Will be Jimmy, Gord, Anthony and ...' An anguished look from Joey. '... Liam.' Ronnie ran down his list. The side was the same as the one that beat Sefton Dynamoes so convincingly.

'Not disappointed are you?' Kev asked Chris. Since

Costello's outburst he was using any excuse to probe Chris.

'Of course not,' Chris replied. 'I didn't expect to get in. Not like him.' He meant Joey. The little fullback looked devastated.

'He's held onto that position a long time,' said Kev.

'He's not going to win in back easily,' said Chris. 'Liam's a cracking player.' He noticed Kev staring at him. 'Something wrong?'

'No, why?'

'Because your eyes are burning a hole in me, that's why.'

'Sorry,' said Kev. He couldn't help it. He was trying to read Chris's mind. If he had heard Costello, he was doing a brilliant job of hiding it. But why would he? Was he headed for an explosion, Krakatoa style?

'Oi,' shouted Ronnie above the hubbub Liam's inclusion had caused. 'When you've quite finished I was still talking.' He ran his eyes over the fourteen players. 'Thank you. We did well against Sefton Dynamoes yesterday.'

'Too right,' said Ratso. 'We were awesome.'

'I wouldn't go that far,' said Ronnie. 'But we dominated play, and we took our chances. It was a good all-round performance. I'll tell you what though, this Sunday we're going to have to be even better. Ajax won again yesterday, keeping their 100 per cent record ...'

'Same as Longmoor,' said Ratso, interrupting.

'So,' Ronnie continued, glaring at Ratso, 'They're on a roll and their confidence is sky-high. We'd be stupid to let them come on to us. They've got the attackers to bury a defensive side. Sure, we keep it tight but the only way we'll keep the pressure off the back four is to get forward as much as we can. That's why I went for

Liam.'

A scowl from Joey.

'He's got the pace and crossing ability to expose Ajax's defence. In short, the emphasis is on attack.'

'Bit of a high-risk strategy, isn't it?' asked Kev. 'I mean, games are won or lost in midfield.'

'Who's arguing?' said Ronnie. 'You all heard me say keep it tight. All I'm saying is we'll get nowhere going route one. You've got to get round the back of this lot.'

Kev shrugged his shoulders sceptically. It sounded like he wanted to have his cake and eat it.

'Not convinced?' asked Ronnie.

'Dunno,' said Kev. 'I just don't want us getting spread.'

'Fair enough,' said Ronnie. 'You and John can have a holding brief in the middle of the park. We've got enough quality in attack as it is.' Conor grinned broadly. As far as he was concerned, he *was* the attack. 'See you on Sunday then, boys,' said Ronnie.

'See you, Ron.'

'Oh, and Kev,' Ronnie said, 'Hang on a sec, will you?'

'What's up?'

'Nothing's up. It's good news.'

'What?'

'It's that scout from Crewe. He liked what he saw. He's coming back to take another look at you this Sunday.'

'You're kidding!'

'I hope you do well. You deserve it.'

Kev was standing letting the news sink in when Jamie came over. 'Walking up, Guv?' he asked.

'Sorry,' said Kev. 'What was that?'

'You all right?' asked Jamie.

'Better than all right,' said Kev. 'That scout's coming

—— 98 ——

back to take another look at me.'

'Fantastic,' said Bashir joining them.

'Jammy beggar,' said Jamie. 'Anyway, are you walking up or not?'

'I'm coming,' Kev replied, 'But do you mind if we take a short detour?'

'Where to?' asked Bashir, joining them.

'Just up to uncle Dave's. Keep Costello and Brain Damage off Chris's back.'

'Why?' asked Jamie. 'Have you seen them about?'

'No,' Kev replied. 'But they're never far.'

'There's no need to nursemaid me,' Chris protested. 'Besides, I might hang on for Dave. He's only here until six today. The aerobics class is off.'

'So is that what you're doing?' asked Kev.

'Might,' said Chris. 'Yes, I think I will. Anyway, what's with all these questions?'

Kev was suddenly defensive. 'How do you mean?'

'You,' said Chris. 'You've been down my ear all evening. Give me a break, will you?'

Kev winced. Maybe he had been overdoing it. But if Chris knew about Dad's part in his old feller going down, how could he be so cool about it? The uncertainty was driving him crazy. It was even taking some of the shine off the news about the scout. 'Fair enough,' he said, backing off. 'See you in the morning.'

'Sure,' said Chris off-handedly. 'Whatever.'

Two

By Tuesday afternoon Chris had had about enough. It was like everybody wanted a piece of him. At home (is that what it was – home?) it was the Taskers. Uncle

Dave and aunty Pat falling over themselves to make him welcome and that excuse for a female Cheryl looking down her nose at him all the time. Maybe this fostering lark wasn't such a good idea after all. The Taskers were all right, but they were always in his face somehow, asking him if he was OK all the time. He was always under the spotlight at school too, what with Spinksy keeping an eye on him and that slimeball Brain Damage acting as public enemy number one. And what was it with the Guv'nor? He'd started out as Mr Nosy and now he was Captain Sticking Plaster. Chris couldn't move without Kev appearing. Now, to top it all, Mrs Burrows had invited herself round for a visit. For visit read interrogation.

'When's she due?' asked Chris as he tossed his school bag in a corner of the kitchen.

'Mrs Burrows?' said aunty Pat. 'About half-past four. Do you want something to eat first?'

Chris glanced at the clock. Five to four. 'Better had,' he said. 'I bet I won't feel like eating afterwards. Do-gooders.' He watched aunty Pat grilling the sausages and smiled. Aunty Pat. Kev had got him saying it. It sounded nice. Like he did belong. 'Where's Dave anyway?'

'Job interview,' said aunty Pat.

'Yes, what sort?'

He detected a moment's hesitation. 'Social services,' aunty Pat admitted.

'What, like Mrs Burrows?'

'Not quite,' said aunty Pat. 'But the same sort of thing. He'd be helping disabled kids.' She gave Chris a wry smile. 'That's right, Dave wants to be a do-gooder.'

'What's wrong with the Community Centre?'

'Nothing,' aunty Pat answered. 'This would be on

—— 100 ——

top. They call it sessional work. An hour here, an hour there.' That's when the bell rang.

'Typical,' grumbled Chris, 'Just when I was looking forward to a sausage butty.'

'You're all right,' shouted aunty Pat from the hallway. 'It's our Cheryl.' Mother and daughter walked into the kitchen together. 'Anyway,' said aunty Pat. 'Where's your key?'

'You gave it to him remember,' snapped Cheryl. She had a way of saying him that rhymed with cockroach. 'I'm still waiting for you to get me a new one cut.'

'Oh yes,' said aunty Pat. 'I forgot.' Cheryl gave Chris a withering look and made her way upstairs. 'Don't worry about it,' said aunty Pat, 'She'll come round.'

Chris grinned. 'Who's worrying?' Ten minutes later he heard the scrape of uncle Dave's key in the lock. 'How was the job interview?' he asked, beating aunty Pat to it.

'Oh, you heard about it, did you?'

'Yes. So? Did you get it?'

'They're going to phone me.'

'I bet you will though,' said Chris. 'You'd make a good do-gooder.'

Dave gave him a sideways look. 'I'm not sure how to take that.'

Aunty Pat laughed. 'I think it's meant to be a compliment.'

They all laughed. It made Chris feel good, all warm inside. The Taskers could be irritating at times, but they really did make him feel like he mattered. That's when the bell went again.

'I haven't stopped answering that door,' groused aunty Pat. 'It's like Lime Street station in here tonight.'

'It'll be Mrs Burrows,' said Chris. It was.

'How are we Chris?'

'We're fine,' Chris answered. 'And how are we?'

Mrs Burrows arched an eyebrow. He was taking the mickey. As usual. 'Settling in all right?'

'Uh huh.'

'Is your room nice?'

'Yes, its OK.' Chris looked around. Aunty Pat and uncle Dave had slipped out, leaving them to it.

'You're probably wondering what's brought me round?'

'No.' Chris had found himself opening up to the Taskers, but he didn't owe Mrs Burrows any favours. They were only apprentice do-gooders. She was the real thing.

'You remember when we talked about your dad?'

Chris felt a rush of excitement mixed with unease. 'Ye-es.'

'Well, he's quite keen for you to visit him.'

'Inside, you mean?'

'Yes,' Mrs Burrows replied. 'In prison. I'll accompany you.'

'But why now? He's never asked to see me before.'

'I think he felt ashamed. Then there's this pride thing. He didn't want you to see him in there.' She rummaged in a cardboard folder. 'This will explain better than I can.' She handed Chris a note which he read in silence. The last line in particular got through to him: *I didn't want you visiting me inside, but I've got to see you. You're all I've got.*

Chris took care not to meet her gaze. 'You won't listen to us talking, will you?' The very thought appalled him.

'No,' she said. 'I'll just take you there. Don't worry, I won't intrude.' Chris rested his hands on the worktop.

It was like he needed something to hang on to. 'Would you like that?'

Stupid question. Like didn't come into it. It was scary, but it was something he just had to do. 'Yes, when?'

'Is Friday all right?' The kitchen walls suddenly seemed to be rushing at him. He felt giddy. 'Chris?'

'Sure,' he said, struggling to maintain his air of indifference. 'Friday's fine.'

Three

Mrs Burrows guided Chris to a table with a couple of plastic chairs. It was one of half-a-dozen tables in a large room. The other visitors looked as nervous as Chris felt. After all, it was a prison. 'I'll be just over there,' she said.

Chris looked up at her. 'Where's my dad?'

'You'll see him in a minute.' With that, she walked to a row of chairs against the wall and pulled out a magazine. That's when the panic set in. It was a dark, creeping sickness that rose from his stomach and filled him completely. He didn't want to do this. It wasn't too late to change his mind. He sat, willing his legs to move. He was about to go over to her when there was a loud buzz and a door swung open. Dad was the third of the group of prisoners to appear.

'Hello there, son.'

Chris settled back into his seat. He'd have to go through with it after all. 'Dad.'

The half-smiling face was strange but familiar at the same time. 'How's things?' asked Dad. 'Settling in at this foster home?'

'You know about that?'

'Of course I do. Your Mrs Burrows told me.'

My Mrs Burrows, thought Chris. As if. 'It's all right.'

'What's the family like ... the Taskers?'

'They're OK. Except for the daughter.'

'Why, what's up with her?'

'She's dead stuck-up. Thinks I'm just a scally.'

There was an uncomfortable silence before Dad picked up the conversation again. 'How's school?'

'You know.'

Dad laughed. 'That's just it, son. I don't.'

Chris tried to imagine what it must be like for Dad. There must be a lot of things you stop knowing. Like what makes life worth living. It was time to make an effort. Dad must have been looking forward to this.

'I've made a few mates,' said Chris. 'I've started playing footy with them on a Sunday. My best friend's a lad called Kev McGovern. He's the team captain ...' He noticed Dad's expression change. 'What's wrong?' he asked.

'Nothing,' said Dad, 'It's just that name, McGovern. Reminded me of somebody. So is this just a bit of a kick-around?'

'No, I'm in a proper league. Well, sort of.'

'How do you mean, sort of?'

'I've only had one game, as sub.'

'What's it called, this team of yours?'

'The Rough Diamonds.'

Dad laughed again, louder this time. 'Good name. Suits a son of mine.'

Chris watched the wry shake of the head. It seemed as good a time as any to tell Dad his news. It wouldn't make him feel any better, but it had to be said. 'I've run into that feller ... Ramage.'

The smile vanished from Dad's face. 'Ramage. How do you know him?'

'His kid brother goes to my school.'

Dad was on the edge of his seat, tense like he was going to leap up and do something. 'Keep away from him, son. Keep well away.'

'No problem,' said Chris. 'I hate his guts. It's mutual.'

'Then just keep it that way,' said Dad. 'And Chris ...'

'Yes?'

'Don't go trying to get your own back. Not on account of me. I've tried revenge and there was only one loser. Me.' Chris didn't reply. 'Don't do it, Chris. Don't even think about revenge.' Chris looked away. 'Did you hear what I said, Chris?'

'Sure Dad, I heard.'

'Promise me,' said Dad. 'You won't do anything stupid.' Chris shrugged his shoulders. 'You've got to keep away!' Dad insisted. 'The Ramages are lethal. I learned that the hard way. Now give me your promise.'

'OK, OK,' said Chris. 'I promise.' Like promises meant anything.

There was a pause, then Dad leaned forward. 'This lad McGovern. Is he in with the Ramages?'

'Of course not,' said Chris. 'He hates them. Why?'

'Oh, nothing.'

There were a few uncomfortable moments before Dad spoke again. 'I don't mean to get heavy,' he said, 'But I made the mistake of tangling with Ramage. That's why I'm in here.' There were more questions about school and the Taskers and even more uneasy silences before Chris asked the inevitable question, more out of habit than expectation.

'Have you heard from Mum?'

Dad looked away. 'You're better forgetting all about your mother.'

'I just want to know if she's been in touch. You said she was in London last time you heard.' That was a year ago, just after Dad got sent down for attacking that copper. The time when everything fell apart.

'Then that's where she is,' said Dad shortly. Chris frowned. This wasn't good enough. 'But has she written? Phoned?'

'No. Like I said, you're better forgetting about her.'

'But I can't,' said Chris. 'She's my mum.'

'A mother's somebody who's there for you,' said Dad. 'That's something you can't say about Annette.'

'Somebody who's there for me,' Chris repeated. 'What, like you?'

Dad's chin sunk down on his chest. 'I asked for that, didn't I?'

'So where is she now?' asked Chris. 'That's all I want to know.'

'It isn't worth it, son. Please, just put her out of your mind.'

'How am I supposed to do that? She's my mum.'

Dad stared back at him for a moment in an agony of indecision. 'You won't like it.'

'I still want to know.'

'She's not in London.'

Chris took the news like a kick in the ribs. 'So where … ?'

'She's here,' said Dad. 'That's right, she's right here in Liverpool. One of my mates ran into her a while back. Seems she met some feller. A club bouncer, or something.'

Chris was finding it difficult to take in the news. It had hit him like a sledgehammer. 'Here,' he repeated. 'She's here?'

'Don't take it too hard,' said Dad, 'She isn't worth it.'

'But here,' said Chris, the tears starting in his eyes. 'She's never tried to get in touch.' His voice broke. 'Not once.'

'Sorry lad, that's the way it is.'

Chris turned and met Mrs Burrows' eyes. He hated her for being there, witnessing his misery. 'Yes,' he said bitterly. 'That's the way it is all right.'

Four

Now what? Chris left school early today. That Mrs Burrows came to collect him. We were on the yard when she pulled up. I wanted to know what was going on, but Chris had hardly said a word all day and he wasn't going to start just for my benefit. I wasn't the only one to show an interest either. Brain Damage and Costello were straight over, sticking their noses in. Honestly, you'd need a can-opener to get inside Chris's mind. He hardly ever gives anything away. There was just that once, when he told me about his dad. And since then, nothing. He's a strange one, that Chris. He's such great company sometimes. Then minutes later he can really turn on you. And what gives with all this secrecy? He didn't even let on he was going early, or anything. I don't know what to make of him at all. The only part of him I seem to be able to make contact with is his anger. And there's plenty of that to go round. Suddenly he's making me really nervous. I should be psyching myself up for Sunday, getting ready to impress that scout, but all I can think about is Chris and the time-bomb that seems to be ticking away inside him. I'm worried, really worried.

Five

Chris was up in his room when the doorbell rang. Downstairs uncle Dave was watching one of the Saturday lunchtime footy shows on TV. The volume was up high. A hint maybe, thought Chris, a finger of sound trying to tempt him down. Uncle Dave wasn't about to beg him, but he wasn't above dangling a footy programme under his nose.

'Chris,' called aunty Pat. 'It's Kev.'

Chris pulled a face. Normally, he would have been glad of the company, but there were all these feelings inside him waiting to explode and he didn't want anyone around when they did. Mum was in Liverpool – Liverpool! That's right, she'd been living right here in the same stinking city and she hadn't come near. Chris listened to uncle Dave talking to Kev, telling him about his new job.

'Two jobs, eh?' Kev said. He sounded happy. 'Watch you don't wear yourself out.'

Uncle Dave chuckled. 'It's not having a job that wears you out,' he told Kev. 'I know. I've been there.'

'If you say so,' said Kev before calling up to Chris. 'I'll come to you.'

'Sure,' Chris said, 'Whatever.' He had to struggle to force out even those two words. It was all rising in him, the sick feeling, the strange, dark fires that swept through him. When he was like this, it was hard to listen to anybody else, never mind talk to them.

'Something wrong?' asked Kev, seeing the expression on his face.

Chris looked away towards the railway bridge, and beyond to the Diamond. 'Why,' he asked, 'Should there be?' He noticed something in Kev's face. He seemed troubled. 'What gives?' he demanded, sensing that Kev wanted to talk. 'Have you got something to say, Guv?'

'No,' Kev replied. It came out as a strangled croak. Not much he hadn't.

'There's no need to worry,' said Chris, forcing himself to make an effort. 'I know.'

This time Kev's face was a picture. Not just troubled, appalled. Chris found it amusing. Fancy being bothered about a little thing like the team selection. Kev ought to have his problems. 'About what you said to Ronnie,' Chris continued.

'Ronnie?'

'When you said I wasn't ready to play a full game yet. It doesn't bother me, you know.' Kev still looked confused. 'That's what you meant, isn't it?' asked Chris. 'Telling Ronnie to leave me out of the starting eleven.'

'Yes,' Kev told him, the penny finally dropping. 'Of course it was.'

It was Chris's turn to be thrown. They were on different wavelengths. Kev was hiding something. 'Doing anything today?' asked Kev.

'No, I don't feel like it.'

'We could go to the Superbowl,' suggested Kev. 'I went there with Cheryl. It's all right.'

'I told you,' said Chris shortly. 'I don't feel like it. Why don't you ask Jamie?'

'Can't. Saturday is the day he spends with his dad.'

'How come?'

'Didn't you know? Jamie's mum and dad are separated. He stays at his dad's flat every Saturday.'

'Bashir then,' said Chris. 'He'll be glad to go.'

'He's out. The whole house was empty.' Kev

frowned. 'It's a bit odd really. There's always some-body in at his. So it's just us two.'

'Just you,' Chris said, correcting him. 'For the third time, I'm not in the mood.'

'Why, what's up?'

'Nothing.'

The troubled look reappeared in Kev's eyes. 'Have I done something wrong?' he asked.

'Of course not,' Chris replied. 'I just want to be on my own.' He was really feeling it now. The build-up inside him. Sickness, anger, frustration. He just wanted Kev out of his room.

'You know, don't you?' asked Kev.

Chris sighed. A long, shuddering breath went through him. 'Now what are you on about?'

'I knew it,' said Kev. 'You heard Costello all right.' Chris didn't interrupt. Where was this leading? 'It isn't my fault, Chris,' said Kev. 'You don't choose your dad.' Still no interruption, but Chris's anger was beginning to have a focus. Kev's father. Of course. He suddenly remembered the way his dad had reacted when he mentioned the name McGovern. 'I don't know that much myself,' Kev continued. 'Just that Dad had a hand in it. Honest Chris, I'd give my right arm for it not to be true. It was the worst day of my life when I realized that Dad was involved with Lee Ramage.'

That's when the dam broke. 'Your dad!' Chris cried. 'So Dad was right. He is in with Ramage!'

The look on Kev's face changed again. Not troubled, not even appalled, he was scared. 'But I thought you knew.'

'You're telling me your dad helped put mine away?'

Kev was backing away. 'Chris, listen to me.'

Chris's voice had dwindled to a whisper. But it was

more threatening than any scream. 'And all this time you've pretended to be my friend?' Chris could hear footsteps on the stairs, but they seemed distant, unreal. First Mum, then this. Why did everyone have to let him down?

'Chris, it's not like that. I wasn't pretending. I am your friend.'

'Drop dead,' cried Chris. 'A friend wouldn't do this to me. Get out of my room.'

Kev stood in the doorway, uncertain what to do. Uncle Dave appeared behind him. 'What on earth's going on?' he asked.

'Ask him,' yelled Chris. 'Ask that rotten traitor.'

Kev didn't stay a moment longer. Turning on his heel, he raced downstairs. Above the pounding of his heart, Chris heard the door slam.

'What's happened, Chris?' asked uncle Dave. 'What was all that about?'

But Chris didn't reply. Instead he walked across the room. Slowly but deliberately he closed the door in Dave's face.

Six

Kev felt even sicker next morning. After calling for Bashir and finding nobody in, he and Jamie went on to uncle Dave's. They almost collided with him on the pavement outside the house. 'Have you seen Chris?' uncle Dave asked. There was an urgency in his voice that worried Kev.

'No, why?'

'Come with me.'

It was with a sinking feeling in his heart that Kev

followed uncle Dave upstairs. 'Good grief!' The lamp was smashed on the floor. All the furniture was tipped over and the bedding shredded. Worst of all for Kev, the team photo he'd given Chris was torn into tiny pieces.

'He's trashed the place,' said Jamie. Kev shook his head. That much was obvious.

'There's something else,' said Dave. He pointed to half-a-dozen sheets of paper on the floor. They were covered with crazy scribbles and drawings, but that wasn't what caught Kev's attention. Over and over again the same thing was written in Chris's untidy scrawl: *Revenge.* 'We were all in bed when the racket began,' Dave explained. 'I thought we were being burgled or something. You know what it's like when you're still half asleep. By the time we realized it was coming from Chris's room, he was gone.'

Kev stared at the mess.

'I suppose you know what this is about,' said uncle Dave.

'No,' said Kev, not quite sure whether he did or not.

'What about that quarrel yesterday?'

'It was nothing,' said Kev. If there was one thing he was learning, it was that lying is sometimes the best policy.

'You sure?'

'I'm sure.' Kev noticed Cheryl standing on the landing by her room. 'I bet you're gloating,' he said. But that's not how she looked. Her face was white.

'That's a bit uncalled for,' said uncle Dave.

'She never liked him.' Cheryl just gazed back at him. She seemed shell-shocked. 'Well, did you?'

'He's right Dad,' said Cheryl. 'Maybe I'm to blame for this.'

'Don't be so daft,' said uncle Dave. 'I know exactly what upset him.' Kev's heart missed a beat. The quarrel. 'And don't worry, Kev,' said uncle Dave, reading his mind. 'It wasn't your little tiff.'

'I don't …'

'Jamie,' said uncle Dave. 'Would you mind, son?' Jamie got the message and went downstairs. 'Mrs Burrows told me to expect fireworks,' explained uncle Dave. 'He went to see his dad in prison.' Kev's eyes widened. 'That's where he was on Friday afternoon,' said uncle Dave.

'He never told me.'

'I'm not surprised. It must have been pretty painful. I don't know how much Chris has said.'

'A bit,' said Kev.

'So you knew his dad was in prison?' Kev nodded. 'And that his mum abandoned him?' Another nod. 'Well, it seems his dad had told him she'd gone away. His way of protecting the lad. All the while he was in care Chris has been telling himself that his mum was miles away. That's why she didn't get in touch. Well, on Friday he found out the truth. She's been just up the road all along. Imagine how he feels.' Kev stared at the floor. He could almost feel the hurt. 'Anyway,' said uncle Dave. 'We'd better go and look for him. I just hope we don't have to involve the police.'

'The police!'

'For his own safety. You've seen the state he gets himself in.'

Kev winced at the thought. 'Me and Jamie will check out Jacob's Lane,' he said. 'I don't think he'll turn up for the game after this, but it's worth a try.'

'Sure,' said uncle Dave, his face betraying his concern. 'Anything.'

'About time,' said Ronnie as Kev and Jamie jogged into view. 'Kick-off's in five minutes.'

Jimmy raced across to add his two-pennyworth. 'Where the heck have you been, Guv? Bashir's already cried off.'

Kev looked inquiringly at Ronnie. 'A family upset,' said Ronnie. 'That's about as much as I know.' Kev didn't let on what he knew. He felt too guilty.

'We've been having kittens,' said Jimmy. 'I thought we had a disaster on our hands.'

'You do,' said Kev, looking around. There was no sign of Chris.

Ronnie's face switched from relief to bewilderment. 'Come again?'

Kev explained the best he could. 'So I've got to look for him,' he told Ronnie.

'You do know that scout has driven up especially to take a look at you?' Ronnie asked. 'He's over there. What do I tell him?'

Kev closed his eyes. Suddenly the world was falling in on him. In all the excitement over Chris he'd actually forgotten that he was being watched in the Ajax game. His big chance, and it had gone completely out of his mind. He felt so cheated. All this time he'd been dreaming of a chance like this, and now that it was within his grasp Chris had snatched it away. For a moment he actually thought of staying. Then he thought of the life Chris had had because of Dad.

'Sorry Ronnie,' said Kev, barely able to force back tears of frustration. 'This is an emergency. I can't stay.' Then came the words he thought he'd never speak. 'Some things are more important than football.'

For a few moments Ronnie just stood there, as if struggling to digest what Kev had said. 'That's all right,' he said at last, 'I understand. Look, here's the best I can do in the circumstances. I'll shuffle the team, make you sub along with Chris. If you do track him down just get here as quick as you can and I'll put you on.'

'Thanks Ronnie,' said Kev. He gazed across at the Ajax players in their red and white kit, then at the scout. For goodness' sake Chris, why today of all days?

'Do you want me to come with you, Guv?' asked Jamie.

'No, you stay here,' said Kev. 'The Diamonds need every man they can get.'

'Go on, Jamie,' said Ronnie. 'You've only got a couple of minutes to get changed.' Jamie nodded and hurried off to the changing rooms.

'Jimmy,' Kev asked, 'You didn't come on your bike, did you?'

'Yes, why?'

'Could I borrow it?' asked Kev. 'I need to find Chris, and sharpish. Before he does something we'll all regret.' Jimmy told him the four-digit combination to the lock. As Kev mounted the bike he gave the scout a last look. There was an ache inside him as big as an ocean.

'Good luck, Kev,' said Ronnie.

'Thanks,' said Kev. 'I'll need it.'

Seven

Kev glanced at his watch and went sick. It was already ten minutes into the first half. 'For crying out loud, Chris,' he groaned. 'Where are you?' He could imagine what that scout would be thinking. Another two-bit scally who knows no better than to throw away his big chance. Even as the injustice of it all was gnawing at him the rain that had been threatening all morning started to drum down. 'Great,' said Kev. 'That's all I needed.' But there was no time to waste cursing the weather. 'Revenge, you said,' Kev murmured. 'But how?'

He'd already checked the Ramage house and the garages. Lee's lock-up hadn't been touched. Next stop South Parade and the taxi firm. As he swung into South Road, Kev found himself pleading with the scout. 'Just wait for me. You've got to hang on.' The line of shops came into view and he hoped against hope that Chris would be there. There was a knot of people outside Ramage taxis. He had to be among them. 'Just be there,' he hissed. 'I can still make it to the game before halftime.' As he skidded to a halt, Kev clocked the crowd on the pavement. On one side stood Dad, Lee Ramage and two of their drivers. On the other, Mr Gulaid, Bashir and the newsagent from further up the Parade.

'Now just calm down,' the newsagent said.

'Calm down!' yelled Lee Ramage. 'Look at my motors, will you? See what he's done.'

Mr Gulaid glowered. 'Don't judge everyone by yourself,' he retorted angrily. 'After what you did this morning you deserve it. But I'm not the one who damaged your cars.'

That's when Kev saw for himself. 'Flipping heck!' All four tyres on Ramage's BMW had been slashed. It was the same story with two taxis parked behind it.

Revenge.

Kev could hear the quarrel continuing behind him, but he was hardly listening. He could only think about Chris.

'Guv,' came a boy's voice.

'Oh, hi Bash.'

'I thought you'd be at the match.'

'So did I, but Chris has done a runner. I've got to look for him.' He managed to look Bashir in the eye. 'Sorry about your van.'

'Why?' asked Bashir. 'You didn't do it.'

'No,' said Kev with an attempt at grim humour. 'But I know a man who did.' He cast a glance in Dad's direction. The look was returned coolly.

'Forget it,' said Bashir, 'I don't blame you for what he does. Neither does Dad.'

'Thanks.' Kev saw Dad heading his way.

'Still taking sides against your own father?' he demanded.

'Meaning?'

'Meaning all this.' Dad indicated the disabled vehicles.

'Mr Gulaid didn't do it,' said Kev.

'Pull the other one; it's got bells on.'

'He didn't!'

An interested look crept across Dad's face. 'Then who did?' Kev shrugged. 'Do you know something? Kev?' Realizing he'd already said too much, Kev jumped on the bike and pedalled away. 'Kevin!'

Neither Dad nor anyone else was going to make him stop. Fifteen minutes left of the first half. But where to look next? Kev was passing the Community Centre for the second time when he heard somebody calling his name.

'Kev.' It was uncle Dave. He pulled alongside and stopped the car.

'Any luck?'

'No, but I've seen his handiwork down South Parade.'

Uncle Dave frowned. 'He's had a go at Ramage's cars. He blames him for his dad getting sent down.'

'Yes, I know the score. I've run out of places to look. You got any ideas?'

'No, I've tried everywhere.'

'Think Kev, we've got to find him.'

'There's nothing. He thinks he's getting revenge for what happened to his dad ...' Kev's voice trailed off.

'Have you come up with something?'

'Maybe,' said Kev, 'But it's a long shot.'

'Anything's worth a try.'

'Then follow me.' Kev stopped five minutes later by waste ground overlooking the junction of Hornby Road and Rice Lane.

'Come on, Kev,' said uncle Dave. 'Give me a clue. What are we stopping here for?'

Kev pointed to a figure squatting on a grassy mound. He was oblivious to the drenching rain. 'That's why.'

Uncle Dave looked down at the traffic backed up along Rice Lane, and nearby, the prison. 'Of course, that's where his dad is.'

'Exactly.' Uncle Dave made as if to get out of the car. 'No,' said Kev. 'Let me try.' Uncle Dave looked doubtful. 'He'll be expecting you to yell at him.'

'Then he's expecting wrong,' said uncle Dave. 'I just want to know that he's all right.'

'And the best way to make sure is to let me have a go.'

'OK, you've got five minutes.'

Kev glanced at his watch. Almost halftime. Uncle Dave didn't know how right he was. 'Chris,' said Kev, approaching the mound.

'What do you want?'

Kev flinched at the resentful greeting. He almost responded in kind, but thought better of it. Instead, he smiled. 'Just being nosy.'

Chris relaxed a little. 'I've messed up, haven't I?'

Kev smiled again. The rage was gone. He'd seen this before. An unstoppable hurricane of anger, then complete exhaustion. Chris's fury had blown itself out. There was a chance. 'Oh, I wouldn't say that.' Chris gave him a questioning look. 'I've been down South Parade.'

'Oh, you saw the cars, did you?' Kev nodded. 'Pathetic, isn't it?'

'You got to Lee Ramage. He's going off his head.'

Chris shook his head. 'Not much of a pay-back for my old feller being in there.' He nodded in the direction of the prison. 'You know what I thought when I got up this morning? I thought I was going to get back at the world – Mum, Dad, Ramage ... your dad.'

'Don't beat yourself up,' said Kev. 'You weren't scared of Ramage. At least you had a go. It's more than most people round here have done.'

'Some revenge. A few flat tyres.' Kev didn't say a word. 'Pathetic,' Chris repeated. 'Everybody must hate me.'

'Who?'

'Your uncle Dave and aunty Pat for a start.'

'What?' asked Kev. 'That uncle Dave.' Chris followed the direction Kev was pointing. 'That's right, he's that worried he's been scouring the whole estate looking for you.' Kev moved closer. 'Mind if I sit down?' Chris didn't actually say no, so Kev sat next to him. 'I meant to tell you about Dad,' he said. 'I just didn't know how.'

'That's all right,' said Chris. 'I think I've just about got my head round it now. What he did isn't down to you. I shout first and think second.'

Kev grinned. 'That makes two of us.' A furtive glance at his watch wiped the smile from his face.

'Something wrong?' asked Chris.

'The little matter of a crunch match against Ajax.'

'Oh no,' cried Chris. 'I forgot.' Then after a moment's hesitation, 'And you came looking for me instead?'

'Yes,' said Kev, 'I'm sentimental that way.'

'Mind if I join the pair of you?' asked uncle Dave.

'Just don't sit down,' Kev advised, getting up. The seat of his jeans was plastered with mud.

At uncle Dave's approach, Chris lowered his eyes. 'Are you sure you want to?'

'The room, you mean?' Chris nodded. 'Forget it, you didn't do that much damage.'

'So,' said Kev, consulting his watch again, 'If the damage wasn't so bad, and everything's more or less sorted ...'

'Go on,' said uncle Dave. 'What are you after now?'

'Could we go to the match? We could be there for most of the second half.'

'I don't ...'

'You'll know exactly where we are. Please.' Kev's eyes met uncle Dave's. You owe me one, they were saying.

'Oh all right,' uncle Dave conceded finally, 'Why not? I'll phone Pat to put her mind at rest.'

'Are you coming along to the game after?' asked Chris.

'I'll do my best, but I want to call in on Mr Gulaid first. Just to make sure Ramage isn't giving him grief over those cars.'

Kev nodded. 'Jump on the crossbar, Chris,' he said. 'We've got a match to win.'

Eight

But by the time Kev and Chris arrived at Jacob's Lane the match was already lost. Or as good as.

'What the … ?' Kev couldn't believe his luck. Against all the odds he'd made it. He'd actually got to the match in time to impress the scout and here was the Diamonds' defence in complete disarray. There was no disguising it, they were making a show of him. And right in front of that scout too. A desperate goalmouth scramble was in progress. Just when he needed them to shine, they seemed intent on committing suicide.

'We're four–one down,' Ronnie informed him. 'And it could just as easily be ten. Jamie and Conor are at each other's throats, especially since Conor scored. Then, to make things worse, Joey's got it in for Liam. It's a nightmare. We're reduced to damage limitation.'

Ajax were peppering the Diamonds' goal with shots. Daz saved with his feet only for Ajax to knock it back in. The big keeper for one was still playing for pride. Even his efforts weren't enough to prevent another heart-stopping moment as a neat back heel by striker Barry Cameron hit the foot of the upright.

'Pinch me,' said Kev. 'Tell me this isn't happening.'

'See that lad?' said Ronnie ruefully. 'Barry Cameron. He's on a hat trick.'

'I can tell,' said Kev. 'He's really going for it. What's that scout going to think of us?' Ronnie cleared his throat and looked straight ahead. 'So where is he?' asked Kev, running his eyes over the sprinkling of spectators.

'I'll tell you about it in a minute,' said Ronnie in a way that had Kev's mind working overtime. The Diamonds had their backs against the wall. Gord cleared the ball only to see it hammered back into the waterlogged goalmouth by their skipper Shaun Lacey.

For the next two minutes it was a free-for-all as shots bounced off heads, backs and shins, or simply stuck in the clinging mud. In the end it was a grateful Daz who went down at the near post to smother a stinging half-volley from five yards out.

'So about this scout,' said Kev, a sense of foreboding beginning to steal through him.

'Gone,' said Ronnie.

'Gone?'

'You weren't here, Kev,' Ronnie explained. 'I tried to get him to hang on.'

'But where is he now?' asked Kev, scanning the other matches. 'I'll find him. Which pitch did he go to?'

'No pitch,' said Ronnie. 'He went home.'

Kev watched Ajax storming forward again and felt his shoulders sag. 'Wonderful,' he groaned. 'Absolutely rotten wonderful.'

'Sorry Guv,' said Chris. 'This is all my fault.' Kev looked blankly at him. 'You must hate me.' Just then he wasn't far from the truth. My big chance, thought Kev. Gone, and all because of you. 'You do, don't you?' Chris started to walk away. Kev watched him for a few moments then smiled grimly. So life's kicked me in the teeth, he thought. What's new? Besides, when it kicked Chris it was wearing much bigger boots.

'Hey,' Kev shouted. 'Where do you think you're going?'

'I thought ...'

'There's a game to pull out of the fire. Don't go bottling out on me now.' Chris didn't know how to respond. He simply stood there open mouthed.

'So you think you can do something?' Ronnie asked Kev.

'I'm the Guv'nor, remember,' said Kev. It was his way. The more bitter the disappointment, the greater the bravado.

'Well, I'm ready,' said Chris, finally closing his mouth. 'Except I've got no kit.'

'Wear Dougie's,' said Ronnie. 'I'm pulling him off.'

'Mine's on under my clothes,' said Kev.

'Then get changed,' said Ronnie. 'I'm putting the pair of you on.' Ronnie withdrew Joey and Dougie in a double substitution. 'Go on, Kev,' he said. 'I think it's a lost cause, but let's see if we can come out of this with a bit of pride.'

A lost cause, thought Kev bitterly, like my life. The self-pity didn't extend past the first minute's hurly-burly in midfield. Within moments the magic of the game was working, its spell surging through his veins.

'What do you call this?' bawled Kev. 'John, Ratso, there's acres of space between you. Gord, Ant, the back four are way too deep. You need to push up.' Then, looking at the front two, he reached deep into the McGovern book of insults. 'As for you two, I've seen lobotomized flamingoes play with more conviction.'

Chris grinned. Was there another kid on the planet who could shrug off disappointment the way Guv did?

'Listen up, Chris,' said Kev, confiding in him. 'The Diamonds are down and very nearly out. We've got to lead by example. I want you to play in the hole behind Jamie and Conor.'

'What about you?'

'See him,' said Kev. 'That's Shaun Lacey. He's running things for them. But not for long.'

The ball came to Lacey thirty seconds later. With all the confidence that comes from a three-goal cushion, the Ajax captain controlled it and looked for options.

That's when Kev pounced, shouldering Lacey off the ball and powering away with it all in one movement. Humiliated, Lacey raced after him.

'Oh no you don't,' Kev snarled, keeping him at arm's length. 'This is mine.' Shielding the ball, Kev spotted Chris sprinting into space to his left. With an impudent flick he put his friend away. 'Chris, Chris.' Jamie and Conor were both making runs, but John was completely unmarked at the far post. Steadying himself, Chris delivered a perfect cross. John was left with a simple downward header. Four–two down.

'Why didn't you pass to me?' Jamie complained.

'I'll tell you why not,' said Kev. 'Because you and Conor are more interested in scoring points against one another than winning the match. Play for the team and you'll get some service. Right, Chris?'

Chris hadn't been thinking anything of the sort. He'd seen John in a good position, that was all, but he knew better than to argue. 'Right.'

'So do the business,' Kev warned, 'Or we'll do it for you.' A couple of minutes later the Diamonds won a throw-in close to the halfway line. 'How long to go?' he asked Ronnie.

'Fifteen minutes.'

'Long throw,' Kev told Ant. 'Give it to Liam.' Bringing the ball down with his chest, Liam drove forward releasing it to Jamie as a defender came in. 'Conor,' shouted Kev. Jamie hesitated. 'Do it!' With a shake of the head, Jamie put the ball in. Conor didn't disappoint, hitting it home on the half-volley. 'So thank him,' ordered Kev.

'Thanks,' said Conor grudgingly. 'It was a good ball in.'

'We're back in the game,' shouted Kev. 'Now concentrate.' Shaun Lacey must have delivered the same pep talk because Ajax were a different team in the closing ten minutes. Space was suddenly hard to come by. 'They've tightened up,' said Kev. 'We've got to ring the changes.'

'How?' asked Chris.

'You drop back into defence. Tell Ant to go forward. We need his height up front.' Chris nodded. 'Liam, John, Jimmy,' said Kev. 'Just knock it forward. Route one.'

'What about pass and move?' asked Ratso.

'Forget it,' said Kev. 'There's no time. Sometimes you've just got to hit it into the box and hope for a break.'

For five minutes the tactic looked doomed to failure as the Ajax keeper dominated his area. Then Liam sent a pass skidding low across the turf. Taking a wicked deflection off Jamie's boot, the ball spun into the air. Unable to believe his luck, Ant lunged forward and headed it in. Four–all.

'Goalazzo!' shrieked Ratso. 'What a comeback.'

But the Diamonds weren't the only ones to have heard of the long ball. Seeing his strike partner driving forward from the restart, Ajax's Daley Bennett launched it. To Kev's horror Shaun Lacey had stolen a yard on Ant. The Ajax skipper was left with the simplest of tap-ins. Ant sank to his knees. Within thirty seconds he'd gone from hero to villain.

'Sorry,' he said. 'I've lost us the match.'

'Get up,' snarled Kev unforgivingly. 'We haven't lost until the whistle blows. Now play Diamonds.' But his team-mates were still reeling from Ajax's surprise strike. Shaun Lacey dispossessed a tired-looking Ratso and punted it forward once more. 'Gord,' shrieked Kev. 'What are you doing? Look at Cameron. Get on him.' But Barry Cameron was away. And with a hat trick at stake he wasn't about to spurn the chance. Chris looked downfield at Kev. The Guv'nor's face was a picture of despair. They'd clawed themselves back into it only to throw it away at the last. 'This is down to me,' he murmured. There was no catching Cameron, but if Daz could slow his advance he might just be able to do something.

'Stand tall,' Chris shouted.

Daz didn't need telling. He rushed out of his goal, arms outstretched. Jinking to the left, Cameron tried to chip him. Daz managed to paw it into the air before crashing to the ground. With the goal at his mercy, Cameron jogged forward to finish the job. That's when Chris saw his chance. Throwing out his right foot he managed to nick it off Cameron's boot and hook it away for a throw-in.

'How long left?' Kev shouted to Ronnie. Ronnie made an 0 with his fingers. They were into stoppage time. 'Come on, lads,' Kev yelled. 'Just get possession and get it up the other end.' He heard the final whistles going all over Jacob's Lane. The Liver Bird team were heading his way. Word had got round that the Diamonds were losing and they wanted to gloat. 'We can't lose,' cried Kev. 'Not in front of that lot.' Brain Damage and Costello were leading the taunts.

'Lose?' said Chris, eyeing the gang, 'Over my dead body.' He was as good as his word, dispossessing Shaun Lacey with a beautifully timed tackle.

'Get it to Conor,' Kev ordered. 'He's free.'

Chris didn't aim the ball. The ref already had his whistle in his mouth. He just hit it with all his might. As Conor ran on to it he was already being challenged by the Ajax keeper. That's when he surprised everyone. Seeing Jamie sprinting into the penalty area he nodded it into his path. Jamie was about to shoot when a covering defender clattered him from behind. The ref blew, but not for full time. It was a penalty.

'Who's taking it?' asked Chris as Conor and Jamie hovered optimistically.

'It won't be either of those two,' said Kev. 'I've only just got them playing together. No sense ruining it.'

'Who then?'

'Me.'

As Kev picked up the ball and placed it on the penalty spot, he was aware of the growing chorus of catcalls from behind the goal. The Liver Birds were doing their utmost to put him off. He gave them a withering glare. That's when Costello came up with his master stroke, producing Kev's beloved Everton shirt from his bag.

'It'd be a shame to see it ruined,' he announced, tugging maliciously at the seams.

'Take the penalty,' said Chris. 'I'll get the shirt.'

'No,' said Kev. 'Leave it.'

'But ...'

'Leave it! Saving the game is all that matters.'

As he stood over the ball Kev watched Ajax keeper Jordan Walsh skipping about on his goal line. The rain had slowed to a thin drizzle and the sun had come out from behind the clouds. Silhouetted against the glaring sunlight, the keeper looked impossibly tall. Arms like an orangutan. Suddenly the goalmouth seemed tiny. No sense trying to place it. As he shielded his eyes, Kev remembered the words of Gareth Southgate's mum in Euro 96: *Why didn't you just hit it?* What the heck, he thought. In this light I'm shooting blind anyway. So that's exactly what he did. He fired it in with all his might. It was a screamer, right into the roof of the net.

'Goal!'

As the ref blew for full time the overjoyed Diamonds converged on Kev. But he wasn't interested in their congratulations. Continuing his run he barged straight into a startled Costello, seizing the shirt. Evading his team mates he peeled away swinging his shirt round his head. He finally skidded to a halt on his knees in front of Ronnie. Ignoring the mud that was now plastering his whole body, he held up the shirt, the side monogrammed with his name. 'I told you Ronnie. I told you they fitted me up.' Ronnie nodded. 'As for scouts,' Kev panted. 'Who needs them? One day everybody's going to know my name.' Ronnie smiled. 'That's right, isn't it Ron? And it'll be for the right reason too.'

That's when the rest of the team finally caught up with Kev. They piled on top of him until the Diamonds were just a mess of muddy bodies.

'That was so cool,' said Chris, flicking mud from his eyes. 'You're an ice man.'

'Feel like you belong?' asked Kev. Chris nodded. 'You should,' said Kev. 'We're your family now.'

Nine

Uncle Dave was jogging up from the car park? 'Sorry I missed the action. I got held up. How did you do?'

'Oh, hi there,' said Kev. 'Not bad, was it Chris?'

'Sound,' said Chris. 'From four–one down to a five–all draw.' Then a downward glance. 'Is aunty Pat angry?'

'No,' said uncle Dave. 'Just relieved. You're paying for the damage though. Four weeks' pocket money.'

'I get pocket money!' exclaimed Chris.

'Yes,' uncle Dave replied. 'You were due the first instalment today.'

'Oh.'

'So you're happy with the arrangement?' asked uncle Dave. 'Four weeks' pocket money to put your room right.'

'Sure,' said Chris. 'I'm happy.' He turned to Kev. 'I am. I'm actually happy.'

'Glad to hear it,' said Kev. 'But what about Mr Gulaid? Lee Ramage was pretty angry.'

'So,' said uncle Dave dismissively. 'Let him be angry. I think he's convinced it wasn't Mr Gulaid who did the cars.'

'So who does he think it was?' asked Chris nervously.

Uncle Dave shrugged his shoulders. 'He hasn't a clue. I dare say he's got plenty of enemies.' There was a twinkle of mischief in his eyes. 'By the way Kev, your dad's asking after you.'

'I bet he is,' said Kev uncomfortably. 'He isn't around, is he?'

'No,' said uncle Dave, 'He said he had business.'

Kev grimaced. 'Figures.'

Uncle Dave produced his car keys. 'Do you want a lift back, lads?'

'I don't think that's wise,' said Kev, inspecting his mud-splattered kit. 'Do you?'

Uncle Dave thought of the seat covers in the car he'd just cleaned. 'Maybe not.'

'We'll walk.'

'OK,' said uncle Dave. 'See you in a bit.'

'Dave,' said Chris. 'Do you mind if we make it about an hour?'

Dave frowned. 'Why?'

'I'd like to see someone.'

Dave glanced at his watch. 'Tell you what, I'll give you a deadline. Let's make it one o'clock. Pat will have the dinner on the table. Fair enough?'

Chris smiled gratefully. 'Fair enough.'

Kev watched uncle Dave making his way across the sodden Jacob's Lane playing fields. 'He's all right, uncle Dave.'

Chris nodded. 'I know. He didn't even ask who I wanted to see.'

'It's called trust,' said Kev.

Chris bit his lip. 'He doesn't deserve the hard time I've been giving him.' Kev chuckled. 'What's with you?' asked Chris.

'You sound just like me. I'm the one who gives people a hard time round here.' He glanced at Chris. 'So what's this you want to do on the way home?'

'I want to see a couple of people,' Chris grinned. 'They deserve better from me too.'

It was Gerwyn who opened the door at the home. 'Good grief!' He picked at the mud on Chris's face. 'And who's this under the camouflage? Swamp thing, the creature from the black lagoon? Why, Chris Power as I live and breathe.'

'Cut the comedy, Gerwyn,' said Chris. 'We've been playing footy.'

Gerwyn inspected their blue and yellow football kits. 'Get away!'

Chris pulled a face. 'Is Crusty in?'

'Yes, he's upstairs nicking the new kid's gear.'

'Not really!'

'No,' said Gerwyn. 'Not really. He'll be glad to see you.' Gerwyn looked at Kev. 'Aren't you going to introduce me to your mate?'

'Oh, this is Kev, the Guv'nor. Dave Tasker's his uncle.'

'Pleased to meet you, Kev the Guv'nor.' Gerwyn and Kev shook hands. It was something that Gerwyn immediately regretted.

'It was muddy today,' said Kev.

'So I see,' said Gerwyn, wiping his palm on his jeans. 'So how's life at the Taskers?'

Chris glanced at Kev. There was a touch of guilt about the look. 'I like it,' he said. 'They trust me.'

'Good,' said Gerwyn, heading for the lounge. 'You deserve it. Give me a shout before you go.'

Chris nodded and led the way upstairs. 'This is my old room,' he said. 'And this is Crusty.'

'All right, Crusty,' said Kev.

'This is Kev,' said Chris. 'The Guv'nor.'

Crusty gave Chris a wary look. 'Hi.'

'So how's things?' asked Chris. 'What's the new room mate like?'

'He thumps me,' said Crusty.

Chris laughed. 'A house rule, isn't it?'

Crusty gave a half smile. 'Something like that? What about your new place?'

'It's good,' said Chris, aware of Kev listening. 'Life's getting better.' There was a pause, as if he was scared of sounding too optimistic. 'Mind you, if you start from the gutter, it's got to.'

'I know what you mean,' said Crusty. 'Still, you sound as if you're on the up.'

Chris shifted his feet. 'You'll get a break sometime, Crust.'

'Don't bet on it,' said Crusty.

That's when Chris flew to the window. 'A rainbow,' he cried. 'A rainbow.'

'Sure,' said Crusty. 'It's a rainbow. So what?'

'So I saw one before,' said Chris. 'I knew it. It was a whatsit.'

Kev and Crusty laughed.

'Oh, a whatsit,' said Kev. 'That explains everything.'

'No, you know what I mean. It's … an omen.' Crusty and Kev exchanged glances. Neither of them got it. Chris watched the rainbow shimmering over the rooftops. 'Don't give up hope, Crust. Never give up hope.'

Ten

Brothers under the skin. That's Chris and me, all right. Neither one of us has really had a taste of the old silver spoon, but we don't go round crying about it. We fight back, always fight back. We even win sometimes. OK, so I took a couple of knocks the last few weeks. The scout business still gets to me. I could hardly sleep last night for thinking about it. The lousy luck, the missed opportunity. It's a funny thing, you know, when there's no hope at all you can just about handle it. It's the little speck of light at the end of the tunnel that breaks your heart. Not that there's much light when it comes to Dad. I've spent the last few days avoiding him. Maybe he's got the message at last. I'm not going to give him the name of the person who did Ramage's motors. I don't grass up my mates. Ever. That's where the winning comes in. Chris seems to be settling in. He's getting a grip on that temper of his. He's even started to smile. I've got a feeling he could be a key member of our squad.

Talking of the Diamonds, Ratso handed me the league table at school today. The positions of the leading pack make interesting reading:

	Pl	**W**	**D**	**L**	**Pts**
	Played	*Won*	*Drawn*	*Lost*	*Points*
Longmoor Celtic	6	6	0	0	18
Ajax Aintree	6	5	1	0	16
Northend United	6	5	1	0	16
Rough Diamonds	6	4	1	1	13

It looks like Longmoor are the season's outstanding side. They're the only team to beat us so far, and the only one to hold on to a 100 per cent record. But there we are at the back of the chasing pack. This time last season we were rock bottom, the licking boys of the whole league. Well, those days are over.

We're a force to be reckoned with. A quarter of the way into the season and we're in with a shout.

Maybe it's the story of my life, the way the Diamonds are shaping up. When I moved to the estate my life had hit rock bottom. I was looking up at the whole world, just about surviving. Twelve months on I've got things I can be proud of. I've got mates who'd go to Hell and back for me. I've got a team that battles right to the final whistle. Yes, and despite my old feller I've got a family who are always there for me.

That's more than surviving. It's living.

Other books you might enjoy in the TOTAL FOOTBALL series

Some You Win . . .

'There's me with my mind full of the beautiful game . . . and what are we really – a bunch of deadbeats . . .'

But Kev has a reputation to live up to and when he takes over as captain of the Rough Diamonds he pulls the team up from the bottom of the league, and makes them play to win . . . every match.

Under Pressure

'The pressure's on. Like when you go for a fifty-fifty ball. Somebody's going to blink, and it isn't me. Ever.'

Kev, captain of the Rough Diamonds, acts swiftly when too many of the lads just aren't playing the game and let pressures off the pitch threaten the team's future.

Divided We Fall

'If you don't take risks you're doing nothing. There's only half an inch of space between determination and dirty play and I live in it.'

That's the law Kev McGovern lays down for the Rough Diamonds on the pitch, but what about off it? When Kev's best mate Jamie's world is wrecked by dirty play he's desperate to get everything back to safe, reliable normal.

Injury Time

'Some people have all the luck. Dave Lafferty for one. How else do you explain a kid who's brilliant at everything? I would have given my right arm to swop with Dave.'

But Kev is stunned when he discovers that Dave has to cope with epilepsy. When he suffers a major attack, the victory the Rough Diamonds are so desperate to win, the longed-for junior league challenge cup, hangs precariously in the balance.

Last Man Standing

'Losing's never fun, but sometimes you learn more from a defeat than half a dozen wins.'

John O'Hara is a mid field player for the Diamonds. Kev doesn't know what to do when trouble at home makes John lose form and credibility both on and off the pitch. His mind's just not on the game, and it's up to Kev to get him back on the ball.